Our Broken World: The Fourth Nightmare

Eight Nightmares, Volume 4

Stuart Tudor

Published by Stuart Tudor, 2024.

This is a work of fiction. Similarities to real people, places, or events are entirely coincidental.

OUR BROKEN WORLD: THE FOURTH NIGHTMARE

First edition. October 31, 2024.

Copyright © 2024 Stuart Tudor.

ISBN: 979-8227773937

Written by Stuart Tudor.

Also by Stuart Tudor

Eight Nightmares
Only My Eyes Move: The First Nightmare
Where Dreams are Lost: The Second Nightmare
Black Masquerade: The Third Nightmare
Our Broken World: The Fourth Nightmare

Watch for more at https://linktr.ee/stuarttudor.

Table of Contents

Chapter One: The Breaking of Reality 1
Chapter Two: The Hammer of Reality 15
Chapter Three: Ashenfall 31
Chapter Four: Our Broken World 54
Chapter Five: The Time the Game was Alive 69

To Alistair, the daft cunt.

Chapter One: The Breaking of Reality

I was there when the last Celestial Visitor abandoned our sorry world. I saw them last in the Dark Lands, a monochrome expanse of shadow and ash, brimming with hostility. We never knew the names of the Visitors, but this one possessed the body of a female mage called Lizzy Northwind. Before she left, I watched her try to fight off a horde of gnawing rats, her firebolts flashing with pitiful weakness against her foe.

Godwin and I spectated this from the grand stone battlements on the north side of Eagle's Cliff. We were fortunate to witness the final Visitor from such a height, we were like cosmic beings in our own right, beholding the end of an era.

Either this Visitor didn't know enough about the rats, or maybe they didn't see the attacking head twitching and separating from the squirming form. But the Visitor found out soon enough. She didn't have time to scream before the rat bites overtook her.

She crumbled to the floor, before disintegrating into ash. The wind blew her remains away.

There was a moment of silence, and a low ominous voice echoed in my head.

Celestial Visitor Lizzy Northwind has departed.

Godwin Dancer: A short muscular man in his black leathery garb of the assassin, strode up to me after the voice faded, his ragged cloak billowing in the breeze. The silence that followed the explosion was deafening, dread sinking in like a stone in water.

"Did you hear that?" Godwin asked, his cheerful demeanor wearing thin and strained. I assumed we shared the same thought: *now that there were no more Visitors, what would that mean for us?*

I just nodded.

Godwin clapped his hands together in what seemed to be resignation, his smile shaking at the edges.

"Bringer knows, it could mean anything," I replied, my mind scrambling to answer the worrying quandary. The Celestial Visitors were always supposed to be there for us. They were spirits from another world, blessing us with their presence and protecting our world from the evil outside by possessing great heroes. Now that they were gone, something had shifted in the framework of our world. Something had been lost.

Godwin strode down the battlements that were usually bustling with guards but were now deserted. We soon found the guards, all dressed in plate mail, clustered in a group and staring at each other in dumb silence, so close there was no space between them.

My skin crawled at the sight. Godwin similarly grimaced upon viewing it. *Were they always like this?* I wondered.

Godwin and I walked through the bustling with the usual crowd of people heading back from work. An unusual silence accompanied the scene. Only the click of the pristine cobblestones underfoot could be heard. The overbearing houses were utterly identical in design and shape, same thatched roof, same brick and wood structures. All the same, clustered so tightly together they could be mistaken for walls.

"Fancy a drink?" Godwin asked, his question slicing through the silence between us like a knife through butter.

"I," I paused. I wasn't supposed to drink; it was one of my vows to The Bringer of the White Flame: Our Deliverer from Evil. I had to consult him about what had happened. "No, I can't."

Godwin shrugged. "Fine by me, would you like a bite to eat instead?"

I paused. My rumbling belly was saying yes, but The Red Phoenix wasn't a place where I should be. The thought of being alone, however, made my skin crawl. "I do need something to eat. I will go inside."

We entered The Red Phoenix, one of many similar bars in Eagle's Cliff that Godwin frequented and that I had only heard about but avoided diligently.

The buzz and chatter of patrons blurred together into a miasma of noise mingling with the smells of beer and smoke. Women of ill repute, which members of my church would be trying to bring to the Flame's saving grace, swaggered back and forth among the patrons. They never seemed to get any customers.

Godwin and I sat at a table. He was glum, like a damp rag, deep in thought. I wanted to leave; the temptation produced by the harlots caused me to shudder.

Godwin leaned back in his chair, and a smile replaced the depressed expression he originally wore. He hailed the barkeep to bring him a beer.

"How are you feeling?" Godwin asked, leaning forward, eyebrows furrowed.

"I am alright," leaning back and heaving a sigh, "I just don't know what this means for us."

A bewitching maiden approached us, asking if we wanted anything to drink. Her tone, that I presumed was supposed to sound pleasant and warm, came off stiff and blank, like a failed attempt to sound human.

Godwin didn't appear to notice, he smiled and asked for a beer.

The maiden nodded and left, swaying her hips in an exaggerated, purposeful fashion.

I wanted to say something, to try to get my mind off the fact that the Celestial Visitors are gone. What did Godwin think of the whole thing, but the words sat leaden in my throat. Godwin drummed his hands on the table, eyes straying over to the women servers.

A young, well-endowed barmaid carried over a large glass of beer, topped with foam, before placing it in front of Godwin. She had a big smile plastered on her face, unwavering and forced.

"Anything to eat, love?" she asked while staring at me, her grin still frozen on her face.

"I will have the beef stew, thank you!" I wanted to keep it familiar. Godwin chuckled and said he would have the same.

"I will also have some more beer," he added, his air still jovial. The woman nodded and she left, her fixed smile never wavering.

"Does she ever stop smiling?" I asked as a shiver went down my spine, watching her unchanging expression. *Why does she never serve anyone else?* I wondered.

"It's part of her job!" Godwin said, grinning a strained toothy grin.

"Like the guards earlier? Was that part of their job?" I grumbled; my idle finger traced the lining of the table. It was deep solid oak, thick with grime from multiple patrons over many years.

"I don't know," Godwin groaned, rubbing his forehead. "I don't know what is happening."

The beef stew arrived after a few minutes, the sauce thick and creamy, the bowls steaming. Godwin and I tucked in, each piece of meat was tender and melted in the mouth. The liquid was positively divine, cooked to perfection. *No wonder Godwin enjoyed eating here, compared to the food from my bare utilitarian quarters.*

One of the women of ill repute sashayed up to us. She instantly began to rub Godwin's shoulder with tender gusto. Godwin nuzzled her hand as he finished eating.

The woman had a distant look. She was like a puppet, performing without feeling.

Godwin didn't seem to care. He caressed her. "Do you want me to love you, darling?" she said, her voice as cold as a corpse.

Godwin winked at me, and got up, hand around the whore's waist. "We will talk tomorrow. I need a... distraction," he said playfully.

"I'm going to The Bringer; He will have answers. Not to mention," I said, watching Godwin continue to fawn over the scarlet woman, "I will pray for you."

"Of course, talk to you tomorrow!" Godwin said, waving to me as he and the whore marched to the rooms.

The cool night air hit me as soon as I left the pub. I inhaled deeply, the satisfying sensation of food in my belly distracted me from the unease of that harlot, the barmaid, and the guards. It was a small relief in such strange times.

I marched towards my church and scanned the ground for any imperfections, any hints that Eagle's Cliff was lived in. There weren't any, the road trodden on by millions of people hadn't a chipped stone.

The Church of the White Flame stood tall and proud like a giant, pale lighthouse. Composed entirely out of white marble, it was a triumph of architecture that never ceased to fill me with pride.

The inside, as was custom, was deathly quiet. Only my footsteps disturbing the moonlit nave. The Bringer stood at the end, an imposing man with arms outstretched, hands open and blazing with the white flame.

The clergy had already gone to bed, and that was ideal for me. I needed some solitude. The main hall was bathed in the moonlight glow, the reds gentle against the white marble. Before me was a statue of The Bringer. His perfect marble hands were outstretched, flame dancing within the palms. I knelt and placed my own palms together in prayer along the oak pews in front of the Bringer. Before his majesty, I was humble. "Bringer of the White Flame, I need guidance. What will happen now that the Celestial Visitors are gone?" My words bounced off the walls, flittering ghosts in the abandoned chapel.

About three days ago, The Bringer would answer me; his voice was deep and fatherly and would provide me with wisdom. I remember that, but ever since then, he has been silent.

I asked him again for a clue, a reason for the cause. But nothing occurred. I begged him for a response. *How could such an important event like this not warrant guidance?* I thought.

"Bringer of the White Flame, please I am fearful of our fate, what happens now, where have the Celestial Visitors gone?"

Nothing happened, with beads forming on my forehead, I continued with renewed fervor.

"Please, send me a sign, I need you in these times."

The statue remained silent, dead as the whore at the tavern. My hands shaking, I closed my eyes and burrowed my head into my praying palms. Against all efforts to not cry again, I called out for another time.

"Bringer, please, just one whisper. I just need to know you are there."

Still, nothing occurred.

I stood up, shaking with worry, and stumbled to my sleeping quarters. As I fell asleep, I found myself thinking, *why isn't my church reacting to this?*

The next morning, as I joined the usual training session, I saw how undisturbed my comrades were by yesterday's events. We were all dressed in our plate mail, complete with helmets to protect our faces.

I fought with my sparring partner in our normal training area, a wide open-air arena encircled with rough stone walls and a dirt floor. The Bringer's blessing saw my sword swing and thrusts burst with white flame, my raised shield summoning domes of white light, protecting me from my partner's blows. Whenever he charged at me, I could leap into the air, landing a short distance behind him.

He never said anything, never commented on how I performed, and never revealed anything betraying a personality. Every time he would charge, he would yell, "Have at you!"

He would grunt before a thrust, groan before a slash. The same roar of fury before he leapt. And he always ignored me. He never responded to any of my questions.

As I paused to catch my bearings during my last jump, my partner waited for me to perform the predictable reaction we had practiced. Instead, I kicked him in the stomach.

He grunted and stumbled back, knocking his helmet off in the process.

What I saw made my hair stand on end.

My combatant was me. The same shoulder-length black hair, the same green eyes, same strong jawline, same height, shoulders, same lips, same everything. My doppelgänger was staring at me, his face completely void of any expression. I ran to each member of my regiment and tore off their helmets.

They were all copies of me, the same picture-perfect copy of me. All gazing in unfeeling, lifeless nothingness.

I fled, my heart pounding in my chest. Mind a-blur, I rushed into the priest's office. I had to tell someone what I had seen. Something had to be done.

Father Gottfried's office was adorned with cold red drapes, fitting for The Bringer's choice. An elderly gentleman that I could always rely on, I found him writing something at his desk. His clothing matched that of the office, the only exception being his white head and beard, the former balding.

"Father, I need your help. Something is wrong outside!" I said, breathless and sweating in panic.

Gottfried looked up, undisturbed, and I quickly realized, lifeless as well. His movements were structured, his mood one of quiet concentration.

"Do you need a blessing, child?" he asked. His voice was a single, fatherly monotone. He stared at me unblinkingly. He remained unmoved at the desk, his writing hand moving independently from the rest of his body.

"Father," I stormed up to the desk, slammed a fist on the table, and glared at him with all the insubordination I could muster. "All the men in my regiment look exactly like me! I don't think they are even real people! What the fuck is happening?!"

There was a chilling moment of silence between us. Gottfried, once such a source of comfort and security in my childhood, was now just an empty vessel. He stared back at me like a fish, his busy hand scribbling nothing on the blank sheet of paper.

"Do you need a blessing, child?" he asked again.

The thought, as random as a knife in the dark, flashed into my mind. All I gave was a low whisper. "Do I even have a name?"

"Do you need a blessing, child?" Gottfried's monotone voice grated on me. I screamed and left the building, rage boiling within me.

There was no direction I wanted to go; I only knew I needed to get away from those vacant copies of me.

Someone waved to me, with no other destination in mind, I approached them.

A somber looking Godwin revealed himself from the crowd, a low grin grew when he saw me. "What's the matter?" he said.

I explained what I saw.

"Every single one of those people," I jabbed a finger at the chapel, "is a copy, an exact copy of me! I..." My head swam from the memory, "I don't know what to make of that!" I gripped my head, still hyperventilating.

Godwin wrapped his arms around me in a tight hug. "It's alright," he said, softly. Godwin let go a little later. My breathing had eased, and the pain in my head had been replaced with a dull sensation of emptiness.

"The whores all behave the same. They never say anything different. It's like they are not even there." After the words left Godwin's lips he started to laugh. I couldn't help but laugh too, despite everything.

"They don't seem real, do they?" Godwin said.

There was nothing to say, I just nodded.

Godwin snapped his fingers, eyes closed. "Right, right, I think I want to explore Ashenfall Academy."

"Why?"

"They might have answers to whatever the fuck is happening here," he said, smiling broadly. His eyes, however, trembled, his body shook as if he was stuck in winter.

"I think I want to pray to The Bringer again, one more time," I said. My head felt leaden, and I just wanted to sleep, wake up from the nightmare that I was in.

Godwin gave a nod. "If you wish, but I don't think the gods are caring."

I snorted before snapping, "The Bringer knows!"

Godwin sighed and gave me a sympathetic glance.

"If you want to join me later, the Far Gates are still working." He pointed in the direction of the town square and started to walk. I joined him, the terror of being alone an excellent motivator.

"Are *you* alright?" I asked after a moment of silence between us. Godwin's shoulders were hunched, filled with stress.

"Just trying to remain positive," Godwin said with a chuckle. "I just don't understand why everyone acts the way they do. He turned to look at me. "Did you also wake up like that? One day everything was off, different from the world you fell asleep to?"

"I only started noticing after I met you three days ago," I said.

Godwin erupted into laughter. "That was a good time. No regrets from me."

We arrived at the Town Square, people bustled, hunting for wares, and sellers yelled over the din of shoppers. At the center stood the Far Gates, connecting us to all corners of the world. Ashenfall was close, about a three-day walk. But with a single step, you could be there instantly. Not to mention you could avoid sundown and the creatures that came out then.

"You were the least stealthy Assassin I have ever seen." A smile was growing on me. Godwin always seemed to have that effect.

Before he stepped into the Ashenfall gate, Godwin turned to face me. "Are you alright?" he asked. His face was a picture of worry.

"I will be," I lied.

"I will keep in contact with you. Will you do the same?"

I nodded, and with that, Godwin marched towards the Gate. One step inside and he was gone.

With panic burning in my heart, I proceeded back to the church. That was when I saw a figure. It was a male humanoid, blazing with pure white light. It was strolling down the street towards the marketplace with the graceful elegance of royalty, someone who is aware of their position in the heavens.

Nobody else noticed The Bringer's Messenger. I ran towards the figure, catching up with him and kneeling before him. Palms upturned in the appropriate gesture.

"Oh, Messenger of The Bringer! Please bless me with knowledge. Tell me what is happening!"

The Messenger glared at me. His hood revealed no face, no eyes, no warmth. His featureless head, burning with blinding brilliance, revealed nothing.

"Please, what is happening? Why have the Celestial Visitors left us? I will do anything The Bringer wishes..."

He didn't say anything, just peered down at my groveling self. "Please, I'm scared. I need guidance from you."

Nothing happened, the Messenger just looked at me with an air of confusion. And he was gone, in the blink of an eye, vanished.

The rest of the town continued as normal; the same repeated conversations blurted out. I didn't move. I had glimpsed the face of God's servants, and he didn't care.

I wanted to cry. Something deep within my soul had shattered. The Bringer didn't seem interested, his Messengers the same. Why had I devoted my life to them if they couldn't be bothered to answer my prayers?

On my journey back, I could see more copies of myself, one a baker, another a pikeman guarding the barracks. There was a blacksmith, the same person as me. They never deviated from their schedule. The baker never stopped baking his bread. The pikeman never strayed from his post, not even to piss or eat. The blacksmith always hammered the steel, cooled it, then repeated the process. It was as if they were not truly alive.

OUR BROKEN WORLD: THE FOURTH NIGHTMARE

Back at the chapel, I collapsed in front of The Bringer and prayed. "Bringer, I need a sign that you are with me. That you haven't abandoned me. Please, just a spark, a flicker, something, anything!"

I waited and waited and waited.

Nothing.

I continued to wait and pray, yet still nothing materialized.

After what felt like hours I got to my feet and dragged myself to my quarters, my mind drowning in a sadness I couldn't describe. I fell onto the bed and stared at the ceiling, listening to the clang of steel and grunts of my regiment. I wanted to cry so much, but my eyes were stubborn. I just stared at the pattern on the ceiling, an endless sequence of flame outlines flowing from each corner.

I thought about my earlier outburst with Gottfried and how he hadn't answered me about my name. I realized that I still didn't know it. I couldn't even remember anyone referring to me by a name.

I clenched my fist in an iron grip. *My name is John*. I decided I would choose my name. *My name is John*.

The clouds cleared from my mind for a moment. The bed was solid underneath me for now.

How are you holding up? Godwin asked, his voice popping into my ears.

My name is John. I said, my own speech reverberating inside my head.

Congratulations! Godwin said, sounding overcome with joy. **Does this make you feel better?**

No, but I need to be different from those other versions of myself. I sighed. Any luck finding anything?

Nope, but I am just finishing off the Guardian. My vision swirled and compressed, revealing Godwin inside a large room filled with bookcases and strange ornaments. He was throwing daggers slick with poison at a tall, robed man, who stood stock still even though he was getting hurt.

The Archmage of Ashenfall doesn't react at this distance. Godwin said with a chuckle, throwing another dagger at the mage. **It will be over soon; I can then explore it thoroughly.**

Good luck. I said, still looking at the ceiling.

Just as Godwin was about to throw the final dagger, something strange happened. The Archmage's neck suddenly snapped ninety degrees. His body contorted, twisting and snapping at strange and upsetting angles before collapsing. A horde of black ribbons laced with numbers burst out of him like a shattered dam.

Bringer! Did you see that?! Godwin cried.

I did! I responded in shock.

It was like something broke... He mused.

Godwin put away the knives and ran over to the body, but in his haste, he tripped over a step and fell headlong into the back wall.

Instead of smashing into it, Godwin fell straight through. Landing with a roll, he found himself in a tight, cube-like room. Ones and zeros flowed along every surface, and in the center floated a comically large hammer.

What the fuck is this... Godwin gasped. I sat up on my bed. Whatever we were seeing, it was important.

Godwin approached the hammer and grabbed it. Almost instantly, our vision was flooded with text, dozens and dozens of words sprawling across our eyes incomprehensibly.

John, come quickly, I think this might be the Gods!

I didn't have to be told twice. I leapt off my bed and raced towards the Town Centre.

I ran faster than I had ever before. While I did so, I saw Godwin's surroundings change, people appearing and vanishing in an instant, mountains, oceans, and skies changing in the blink of an eye. This was how the Gods originally made the world, the chaos that birthed it, this hammer, whatever it was, yielded the power and the voice of the Gods.

I threw myself into the Gate. The flash that should have happened, the deadening of sound that preceded the rush of air into the new location didn't manifest. Instead, I fell with a clang onto the cobblestone on the opposite side of the gate.

Dazed, I got up and tried again, the same thing occurred.

Godwin, something is wrong with the Gates. What should we do?

Godwin tried to pull the hammer with him. But it refused to move.

Shit, I don't know, it's three days away on foot from Eagle's Cliff.

Godwin tugged on the hammer one more time, before letting go with a grunt.

Alright, I will make my way back, wait until I arrive.

I turned to leave when something clicked in my mind.

What if I met you halfway? I said, I can walk to you!

Alone might be too dangerous. Least of all for a chunky man like you. I can sneak back without too much trouble.

How about other Gates? I said. I could try them!

Godwin smacked his forehead, **Bringer, that could work, go to the East Gate.**

Say no more!

I ran faster than I thought possible, the world around me a blur of sellers and buyers, of guards and their swords. All worthless except for the chance of getting to this Hammer, our ticket to the answer to whatever was happening.

The East Gate was situated in the industrial district of Eagle's Cliff. In the center of the overbearing carpenter woodshops and steel mills, stood the Gate, awaiting me.

Nobody paid attention to me as I marched up, all too busy with the menial tasks of the day.

I stepped into the Gate, heart pulsing with anticipation. *Please let it work, please let it work.* I thought.

As easy as taking a walk, I entered one side and left on the other. No flash or rush. It was as consequential as walking through a sheet of blue.

The heavy weight of sadness hung over my shoulders, an anchor wanting to snap my neck.

That's weird. Godwin said. He watched with confusion as I attempted to enter the Gate again. But nothing changed. **I wonder why they are not working.**

I stood still, head drooping, the walls of the industrial complex clustering around me, entrapping me among the lifeless.

John? Godwin said. **Are you alright?**

I will be, I said.

Godwin's smile cracked before repairing itself.

Just wait there, I am on the way back, expect three to four days.

I guess we have no other choice. I sighed, defeated.

Don't worry my friend, it will be alright. Godwin assured.

Keep in touch.

When I returned home, I fell back onto my bed and stared at the ceiling.

Chapter Two: The Hammer of Reality

The days blurred together, and a haze of doom and worthlessness cocooned me throughout. Sometimes Godwin's voice would call out for me, asking if I was okay. I would always say yes, all while looking at the ceiling.

Godwin would show me pictures of his journey back. People, the land, reality itself, seemingly breaking. Buildings flickered in and out of existence. Formerly normal creatures contorting into something much more grotesque and bizarre. People behaved in ways that defined all logic.

We agreed on the term: The Breaking. It just stuck as appropriate.

I just lay on my bed. Despite my rumbling stomach I never got hungry, I never got thirsty or tired. I just remained unmoved, simply watching the pattern, unwilling to do anything else.

"Greetings John!" Godwin said, climbing into my bed-chamber window. I didn't move.

He landed on the floor with cat-like grace. "I know things look bad at the moment, but if we hurry now, we can use the hammer."

"Is it as bad as you say it is?" I asked, still as a statue. The endless grunts and clangs of my copies outside tore at my ears. I hated them with a boiling passion.

Godwin paced around the room, stopped at the center, clapped his hands together, and said, "Come on John, we have a chance to talk to the gods. If things continue to break, then we might not have much time."

I groaned and sat up. "Alright, Godwin." I was already exhausted, but for him, I would do it.

"I believe I have supplies," I said, rummaging inside my satchel. I found four sunflask healing bottles; it will be enough for now. "How many sunflasks do you have?" I asked, shrugging the satchel across my shoulders and putting my helmet on.

Godwin checked his bag and pulled out four flasks. He winced before putting them back.

"Shall we get going?" He asked.

"Sure," I replied, not bothering to lock the door; this was the last time I would see this hollow city.

The road in which I lived was filled with ordinary people going along their scripted routes. The cobblestone paths were, however, unscuffed and polished.

The sun shone on the high marble walls that supposedly kept us safe from outside threats. The collection of wood and stone houses and stores grew and clustered around them in perfect symmetry. They were carefully designed to look as picturesque and pleasant as humanly possible.

We weaved through the crowd, who all spoke their lines perfectly, and on repeat over and over again.

I noticed that only some behaved as they should.

An old beggar woman spun around in place. Her movements froze as if paralyzed in a simple hand wave, her expression one of static joy.

A young soldier walked into the wall and continued despite the obstruction. The wall was smeared with blood as he ground his face into it. He groaned and gurgled as more and more of his face crushed into the wall.

"Godwin, I think the city is becoming affected by the Breaking," John said.

"Don't touch them, don't go near them. We don't know if it spreads."

The crowd grew as we headed towards the front gates. More and more unaware people were lying on the floor or walking in place, stuck in the walls and in each other. They squirmed inside the walls, slick with blood and guts as their bodies were sliced into the brick and marble. Those unfortunate enough to be broken into each other were an unholy mass of bodies. Some screamed, some groaned in pain, while others mumbled their lines, ignorant of their apparent agony.

At the city gates, we encountered a scattering of Broken people. They stood perfectly in place, babbling over each other. Their arms and legs twitched in contorted staccato movements. The heads shook from side to side at such a speed they blurred together. Limbs and bones snapped in their contortions; they howled like tortured dogs.

"Remember, don't let them touch you," Godwin said in a harsh whisper. He pointed to the open gate. "We just need to get through these Broken. Don't panic." He said in a trembling voice.

I breathed in and followed Godwin into the crowd.

A barrage of voices hit me from all sides. They droned with inane nothingness. The Broken people's movements were seemingly more erratic with each moment that passed.

Godwin, living up to his surname of Dancer, ducked and weaved in between the strange Broken people. I could only just keep away from the knife-like arm movements. A Broken person kicked out suddenly and nearly hit my shin.

Impatience was growing within me. *There needs to be a way to get through this more quickly, without taking a risk*, I thought.

I took my shield in both hands, and I smashed it into the nearest Broken.

The shield collided with the person with a dull fleshy smack. The Broken person fell and began convulsing on the ground. Blood rising within me, I smashed my shield into another, and another, and another.

Godwin shouted and rushed back towards me. I had carved a way through the crowd, and the gate was in sight. The Broken people lay on the floor, vibrating and bending at unnatural angles. All I cared about was getting to the Ashenfall Academy.

Godwin knocked the shield out of my hand.

"What in the Bringer's name do you think you are doing?!" he shouted, panting from what was more horror than exhaustion. "You could get infected!"

"Look at me," I said. I picked up my shield and held it up for Godwin. Nothing was out of the ordinary. "I don't think anything is wrong with it."

Godwin peered at the shield, as one would do when looking at a dog that might bite them.

"Maybe it doesn't spread through touch," Godwin muttered, his face brightened a bit. "Perhaps we don't have to be too careful with the Breaking?"

I lowered the shield. "Maybe not."

"Nicely done then," Godwin said. There was a rumble, a growing chorus of voices behind us within the city.

Before me lay the once emerald hills of Outskirts, now obscured behind a mass of buildings, farmhouses and guard outposts sinking through the ground, phasing in and out of existence, vanishing for a second before reappearing like nothing had changed.

Clanging metal and shouts of "Murderer!" rang out, footsteps thundered toward us. I didn't want to look back. Godwin leaped forward and slashed the chain holding the gate up. He rolled to my side just as the gate crashed down.

"You might have started a riot, or have called the guards on us," Godwin said, grimacing. "That should keep them away from us for now. But I think we should keep going."

"How much time have we got before nightfall?" I asked, replacing the shield on my back.

"A couple of hours," Godwin said, "then we should make camp for the night. The creatures that come out are too strong and mutated. We need to get as close to Ashenfall before nightfall."

"Disfigured?"

"Breaking does terrible things to their bodies, like those townsfolk. Sometimes it's much worse, such as their bodies twisting into something abnormal." He strode down the King's Road as he spoke.

I quickly joined him before I could think too much about the creatures that lay ahead. The sky was in parts, either pure featureless black or a sickening display of dark purple. These abnormalities were cut in perfect squares, jarring in the otherwise normal clean blue sky.

I stared, horrified by the sky. There was a sense of helplessness against being in a world abandoned by our true Gods. *Suppose they were even more than just observers of our existence.*

Godwin broke me from the trance with an arm across the chest, stopping me in my tracks. He pointed to a giant rat, normal, except for the occasional spasm. The head would twist one hundred and eighty degrees at random.

"Those rats will give you extremely high knowledge if you kill them," Godwin whispered as if he were hunting a dragon. "We can become as strong as an experienced Celestial Visitor."

"As long as we don't get bitten," I said.

I drew my sword, tiptoed to the rat. I couldn't stop the smirk that ran across my face, it was so comical to me, trying to sneak up against a rodent as if it were something much worse.

I slashed it in one quick strike.

The head snapped back behind, its pale pupil-less eyes goggled at me just as the sword landed directly between the eyes. It screamed a grating, distorted howl. Its head convulsed rapidly back and forth.

The rat collapsed, ribbons erupting out of its head, still twitching as it disintegrated.

I was hit by a rush of energy, a surge of power that I couldn't quite understand. It was like I had glimpsed a part of heaven and saw what awaited me.

A blinding yellow light dazzled me before I found myself back in my world.

My body throbbed with newfound energy and power. But then the elation faded, and the strength I thought I had acquired, disappeared.

"Feels good, doesn't it?" Godwin said with a smile.

"It did, but I don't feel anything anymore," I said, flexing my hands in confusion.

"What do you mean?" Godwin said, his brows furrowed in uncertainty.

"I touched heaven but can't do anything I couldn't already do."

Godwin vaulted over me, throwing daggers into another rat. A blinding light engulfed Godwin, who briefly levitated off the ground before it faded and sent him back to Earth.

Godwin, flushed with joy, a brief happiness that was soon replaced with confusion and drooping disappointment.

"I don't understand this," Godwin said, thrusting his hands forward as if trying to throw something. "I should be more powerful; why can't I throw that fire dagger like the Visitors?"

"I... don't think we have that privilege," I said. "It would seem that the Gods aren't going to ordain us with Knowledge. Maybe only Celestial Visitors are allowed to do that?"

Godwin stood, shaking with either fear or distress. The sun sank into the broken sky, the only regular aspect left in the heavens.

Should I comfort him? I thought before Godwin snapped up straight and let out a low moan before saying.

"Then let's get going, the sun is going down, and we need to be as close to Ashenfall as possible before we camp for the night," Godwin scooped up his satchel.

"Agreed." A dull pang of guilt throbbed in my gut; I should have comforted him.

We continued walking. Bandits who would have otherwise tried to ambush us lay on the floor, stiff as a board. They didn't react to us; they were too Broken.

"How did we let this happen?" I asked.

"What?"

"What did we do to get abandoned by the Gods?"

Godwin shrugged. "It could be anything. Maybe they and the Visitors got bored of us and are throwing us out."

"But they could have given us an opportunity, right? To prove ourselves worthy?"

"I doubt they even think we are worth that," Godwin sighed.

"But why now?" I pushed.

Godwin didn't answer. He pointed a finger in front of us. I didn't see what he was gesturing at until an elongated form slithered out of a nearby bush.

It was once human, but now its body seemed to have been stretched out. It more resembled a snake with human limbs and a face. The limbs moved as if they were walking like a human. The features were painfully stretched across his face. It groaned as it slither-walked. The metal armour it wore had stretched to fit the body it now had, and its sword and shield scraped against the

ground. The setting sun caused the knight's skin to glisten with pustules of sweat.

A wave of disgust hit me when I saw that creature. "What in the Gods happened to that thing?"

"I think it Broke. That does strange things to the body," Godwin said, equally disgusted by the beast. "I say we sneak past it, play it safe until we get to the first Guardian."

"The sun is setting; it would be foolish to keep skulking around. We are moving too slow." I protested.

Godwin shook his head. "This is the shortest route." He slipped off his backpack, laying it carefully without a sound.

The creature stalked around, not paying attention to us in the slightest.

Godwin tiptoed towards the monster, daggers drawn, waiting to pounce.

He leaped and sunk a dagger into the Broken knight's head.

It unleashed a garbled scream, one vaguely that of a human male. Dozens of black ribbons, laid with ones and zeros cascaded out of the creature's head and into the weird sky.

The creature collapsed; the force of the ribbons knocked Godwin back. Dropping my backpack,I raised my shield, producing a thin translucent platform, catching him as he fell.

Godwin rolled off it with the ease of a cat, landing on his hands and knees. He scrambled to his feet, standing up with a theatrical bow.

"Well done!" I said, lowering my shield and letting the platform disappear.

"Thank you, thank you." Godwin grinned. The smile quickly faded when he saw how low the sun was getting. "Shit," he pointed at the faded dusk.

The sun disappeared, and pitch-black darkness swallowed us up. At certain angles, the darkness would disappear and reveal the landscape as if it were midmorning.

Godwin's eyes widened, and we sensed the near-animal monstrosities roaming the fields. We gathered our backpacks in silence, only the wet slap of the knight flopping on the ground to accompany us. Eventually, that too disappeared into the dark the further we walked.

We marched without saying a word or looking at each other. I watched the patchy, breaking sky.

How much time do we have left? I wondered as more of the sky broke, turning into squares of unnatural colour. Soon there will be only a broken sky. I forced back the tears; I was weak now, and whoever watched over us, would not care if I was vulnerable or remorseful. Weakness will not win us our lives.

"Do you hear something?" Godwin asked, head snapping back, picking up some strange sound.

I was about to answer, before I heard it too.

A garbled screech came from behind us, akin to a strangled owl. Godwin, now pulling out a torch, followed the sound.

A swollen barn owl, the size of a large dog, dragged itself on the ground towards us. Its wings pulled it towards us in stiff, abrupt motions scraping its face against the floor.

I stared, fascinated by the creature, at how mutated it had become, and why it had any interest in us. Then a hand fell on my shoulder, sending a jolt of panic through me.

"John, we have to go," Godwin said; a wolf howled in the distance.

"I... I will watch your back," I said. "Please give me the torch."

The owl was less than a foot away; Godwin handed me the torch. "Keep close to me, the Guardian area is pretty close."

With my shield strapped to my back, I took the torch in one hand and held my sword in the other.

The owl let out a bark like a choking dog; it flew at me in a single static movement, floating in the air as invisible claws slashed at my helmet, its head stained with blood from how it had been moving.

Godwin pulled me along with him; I swung the sword and hit the frozen owl, slicing off a wing. It tumbled to the floor and began to convulse as it was absorbed into the earth.

I turned around and chased after Godwin, hearing a deafening roar from the right side. A living statue of a grizzly stood frozen on its hind legs, its roar on repeating loops, seeming to start before the last one ended. I was flung back by an unseen force, and the frozen bear slid towards me, still reared up, waiting to strike.

From within the darkness, Godwin leaped onto the bear's back and slashed his knife around the throat.

The Broken roar ceased instantly, and the rigid frame sagged like the body had lost all its bones. The explosion of ribbons signaled its end.

Godwin pulled me up. Thanking him, I chugged a flask leaving three remaining. The darkness had gotten thicker, impenetrable and completely silent.

Before Godwin and I could continue our journey, a disjointed bark sounded from our left.

In a single motion, I pulled my shield from behind my back and held it toward the direction of the sound. I dropped the torch, creating a small dome of light around us, I waited, bated breath for whatever was out there.

I had meant to shield both of us from whatever was about to attack. What I didn't expect was my shield to extend to a sharpened point before me.

A dog-like yelp came out from the darkness.

"Thank you," Godwin said, chest heaving and sweating. "But how did your shield do that?"

"I don't know; I think the shield is Broken." The extended shield vibrated and twitched, no heavier than it usually was. The light revealed a wolf with an upside-down head, contorting and shaking with impossible speed. Completing this grim picture was boxy blood that pooled around the elongated shield.

I moved my shield in a shrug motion, uncertain of what else to do. It retracted in a flash and the wolf flopped to the ground.

Another roar echoed in the dark, followed by vaguely human gibbering.

Godwin's initial shock at the shield vanished into stoic determination.

"We run! We can figure out things later!"

Godwin grabbed my arm and pulled me forward; the nonsense mumbling had gotten louder, including the pain ridden groans of creatures piling toward us. Owls, bears, wolves, and whatever the babbling animals were. We had taken too long.

In the flickers of the firelight, I caught glances of what was chasing us.

They were humanoid, nearly invisible aside from outlines that betrayed their former humanity. They were armed with knives, swinging in erratic motions. They would slide along the ground like the ghosts they resembled, their legs stuck together.

The sound of screaming men and women clashing steel joined in the chorus. The townsfolk, the ones I angered back in Eagle's Cliff, were still chasing after us.

The strange creatures within the darkness attacked them. They didn't even notice as they were cut down.

"Well, that was lucky!" Godwin said wryly between pants.

"I suppose I did well after all!" I chuckled, beaming with pride.

"Either way, we made it," Godwin said, panting. We had run up to an archway, a fog swirled inside it.

Without a moment's notice, Godwin pulled both of us through the fog wall.

We switched from night to day in a single second. A wide, dusty field stood before us, bereft of life except for a person. Two men were in the area, one lying in a bloody, mangled heap on the ground; the other bashed his victim's head in with a rock. The assaulter, clad only in a loincloth, grunted with each strike.

He turned to face me, a look of savage rage in his eyes as he began to walk forward. One hand held the bloody stone while the other dragged the second man's corpse. Then, finally, the strange announcer cried out:

Khan: The First Murderer.

"Come, brother; you will have your use yet," said Khan.

The monsters stood, slashing and killing each other inches from the archway, unable to cross the threshold.

Godwin raised his weapon; I did so as well.

"I will bash you like this spoiled brat!" Khan yelled, his head twitched and bent at unnatural angles.

Godwin's eyebrows raised as if remembering something. He dropped his satchel and produced a pile of simple metal traps.

"If I can lay these, we might be able to finish him off quickly. Distract him while I set them up!"

My blood chilled at the thought of the fight, but I could do nothing now but confront Khan.

I nodded, and Godwin ran along the right-hand side; I raised my shield high, sword at the ready. Sweat was already beginning to bead on my forehead.

Khan raised the bloodied body of his brother in the manner of a crude fleshy hammer, growling like a feral beast.

I dodged and rolled in opposite directions to avoid the slams. I thrust my sword forward into Khan's thigh, sinking it in deep.

"Spoiled bastards!" Khan roared, slamming his brother's corpse to his right, striking Godwin-who let out a yelp in response. The corpse somehow had remained intact despite all logic to the contrary.

My hand steady, I sliced a horizontal arch at his left leg. The cut sunk deep, spilling box-shaped blood onto the ground.

I parried another blow from the corpse. "Run to me now!" Godwin shouted. Looking from side to side, I spotted him waving to me, a pile of metal traps glowing with red-orange colors.

Khan raised his other hand, about to throw the rock he had used to kill his brother.

The clang of the rock bounced off my shield, firing back at Khan's head.

A strangled eldritch cry followed. I paused, lowering my shield as Khan's body collapsed to the ground, twisting and contorting into strange formations — a blood box formed around the bloodied stump that was once his head. A flurry of ribbons flew out of Khan's neck stump before his body sank into the earth like a stone in water.

After what felt like hours, the omniscient voice appeared:

GUARDIAN SLAIN

Godwin cheered, hysterical with joy despite bleeding from open wounds across his head and chest. "We did it!" he shouted breathlessly. "We did it!" He didn't seem to be in any pain, or perhaps he was only ignoring it.

We hugged and Godwin drank one of his Sunflasks, his wounds disappearing instantly. "And we didn't have to use the traps!" He said, flushed with joy as we gathered them up. Afterward, we walked to the door towards Ashenfall. In the blink of an eye, we were back into blinding darkness.

There was a single unlit campfire, centered perfectly in the middle of a circle where one might rest for the night.

"We can get there tomorrow," Godwin said. I just nodded, unsure of what to say. Godwin in the meantime, pressed a hand to the dormant campfire and it cracked into life.

We set up camp around the fire. The sparks that flew off drifted into our flasks, refilling the used ones with liquid-nourishing flame.

"Godwin," I asked as we ate some of our rations, "how do you feel about our chances? Do you think that this hammer will save us from The Breaking?"

There was a pause; Godwin's arms shook before the smile returned. "If I were not optimistic, there would be nothing to hope for." He shrugged as though he were trying to appear indifferent. "I saw that thing create new people, level and change rooms and force away the Broken!"

"But can *we* use it?" I asked. I was looking at the forest floor, the sadness coming back again.

"No, but I heard the gods through it; they were speaking to each other about ways to fix our world."

My head sprung up, the sadness shrinking away. "Were you able to talk to them?"

"I tried, but they wouldn't stop talking to each other while I held onto the hammer." Godwin shrugged, "Not a problem, but with things getting as bad as they are, I wanted to make sure both of us were close to the hammer."

"Thank you, Godwin," I said, fighting against the bubbling sadness.

"I hated being alone. The world is so cold and empty, I am sure you can relate."

"More than you know, my friend," I said. I handed him some of the stew. "As a thank you for not abandoning me."

"I appreciate the gesture," Godwin said, beaming joyfully. After a moment eating, he continued. "It's a damn shame you refused the whores I gave you." He said, chuckling.

"I feel like an idiot forever thinking The Bringer was real," I grumbled. "This world feels alive, but so vacuous."

A strained chuckle came in response. "But it's the only one we have."

There was a pause; Godwin stretched. "I don't know why the gods tricked us with a false idol, nor do I understand why they don't care. But maybe your faith in the real gods can sway them."

"I don't know," I muttered.

The atmosphere grew glum, like there was a fog of sadness over us. Godwin's big, toothy smile brightened up the campfire.

"Do you remember when you tried to take me to prison?"

I snapped my fingers. "Yeah, you broke out of the cell within the hour."

"Those bars were weak as shit." Godwin laughed. "I don't think they were ever designed to be broken out of, I swear the bars were made of soft rubber."

"Did I ever tell you about my fondest childhood memory?" I said, the words bursting from my mouth like a broken dam.

Godwin cocked a wry eyebrow. "You didn't. Please share." He rolled his hand out in an extravagant gesture.

I straightened myself up while seated cross-legged at the warm, nourishing, safe flame in front of me.

"It was when I was ten. My father and I went fishing by the lake in my village." A tear formed in my eye. "It was the last time we spent together before the knolls raided us."

"He always taught me to believe in The Bringer, to bring his flame to the land. He would show me how to swing a sword, to pray for The

Bringer's deliverance, and how to protect the innocent. He helped me enlist here."

"He sounds like a good man."

"He was." I ran my hand over my face, carefully wiping away the tears. "But there is this terrible thought that he wasn't real. That my family back home is just like everyone else in Eagle's Cliff." I heaved in a deep breath. "Do you feel that too?"

"Of course, I remember when I was a street urchin, I picked some rich sucker's pocket, only to discover it was some great assassin-type man who decided to take me in." Godwin chuckled. "We killed our first nobleman in a group effort," he sighed wistfully. "Good times."

His expression suddenly became very solemn. "It feels like that's all that counts. I know he is real because he feels real."

The thought of my father lingered, my breathing became quick and heavy. He had to have been real, otherwise I never would have had a father, a mother or a life, really had a life. My body started to quake, the desire to curl up into a ball and just hold myself, to assure myself I was real.

"Hey," Godwin pulled me back from whatever hell I was spiraling into. He was offering me a single piece of chocolate.

"Take it, please."

We were only supposed to have one piece of chocolate a year, on The Bringer's birthday. My mind drew a blank on the date.

I stared at the chocolate with stinging guilt. But maybe, just maybe, there was a chance The Bringer was working through Godwin.

"Don't worry, it won't kill you," Godwin said, his voice playfully sarcastic.

I plucked the chocolate and ate it. The sweet taste provided some momentary relief. It was real. It had to be. *Why didn't I bring chocolate with me?* I thought, the guilt dripped away, replaced with icy irritation.

"Thank you," I said, the sugar sprouting a smile on my face. "I will get us some more in Ashenfall."

"Remember, we look out for each other." Godwin yawned and continued to poke the fire. "Are you alright to sleep?" he asked.

"I will be okay, thank you for asking."

"Then I suggest we get to bed now," Godwin lay down on his bedroll and squirmed on his back, before finding a comfortable position. "We have quite the journey ahead, and Bringer willing, things will remain predictable."

"He will," I said, finding that comfortable spot on my own bedroll. "Good night, Godwin."

"Good night, John," Godwin said.

I lay awake for hours. *How many days left did we have?* I thought as I drifted off to sleep. *Will they be any worse?*

I tried to ignore the garbled groans and contorted snarls of whatever lurked outside the safety of our flame. I was lulled to sleep by Godwin's snoring.

Chapter Three: Ashenfall

The morning had come, although the sky had now fully Broken into a hazy mixture of bright pink-purple stripes.

We cooked breakfast, a simple meal of meat and nuts washed down with wine. My belly pleasurably full, and I, sated with courage from the wine, we packed up.

"Let's get more supplies in Ashenfall before the next Guardian," Godwin said.

I paused. "How many do we need to get through?" I asked.

"Two more before we can contact the gods, if they would listen to us," he said. His smile was highly strained.

"They will answer us?"

"Yes." His voice was final, no argument would be tolerated.

I stared at the campfire as it burned with an ever-dimmer flame. Soon it would go out and need to be reignited.

"Let's get inside the walls so we won't have to worry about hostiles," Godwin said.

"Why do we have to go through the Guardians anyway?" I asked, "Can't we just march straight there?"

"Unfortunately, no, our world is designed like this; not even the Celestial Visitors can avoid the fights with the Guardians. It's what we do to move through this plane. I did it before hunting the hammer and now we do it again."

Was it always like this?

I tried to think back to the time before I became aware. But it appeared to me in a blur, a happier time, blissfully ignorant of our real unreality.

"Why did you put the buckets on their heads that day?" I asked,

Godwin shrugged. "I didn't want people reacting to me stealing from them, I needed food."

"Was that when you figured out that people weren't behaving properly?"

"Maybe..." Godwin groaned, "I just didn't want to admit to myself."

"You tried to put a bucket on my head!" I said, the memory brightening my mood for a moment.

"Only because you weren't behaving differently," Godwin nudged me in the ribs.

There was a moment of silence. Ashenfall rose up before us.

"Anyways," Godwin continued, "It was pretty funny to see, you were very confused."

"We were never trained to deal with bucket assaulters. It was new for me!"

The road up to the high walls of Ashenfall, a place designed to look as glorious and powerful as Eagle's Cliff. The walls were pristine and clean, sparkling like diamonds. *Maybe the Broken hadn't gotten into Ashenfall,* I thought. It was a small hope that was lost upon seeing the town guards.

"Oh no," Godwin gasped, my stomach heaved at the sight.

The guards were stuck in the walls, sliced in half, walls soaked in blood as they stared unblinkingly, smiling at us as we came up. They tried to move, tried to wave, perhaps. But they couldn't. Their arms seemed to have been set in stone.

I tried not to look at them as Godwin picked the lock, that didn't prevent me from feeling their hollow glares.

"What do you think you are doing?" one guard demanded, twisting feebly in an attempt to intervene. But there was no escape from their prison.

I wanted to put them out of their misery, a quick stab to end their mindless entrapment.

I drew my sword and strode towards the first guard to my right, who squirmed and barked for me to show my pass.

Godwin grabbed my arm.

"If you kill him, we will start a riot like at Eagle's Cliff."

"Am I just supposed to leave him here?" I choked back the tears threatening to form. "Can't I give him the mercy of death? He's encased in stone, for Bringer's sake, he's being torn apart!"

I stamped toward the guard, my sword drawn and ready to end his suffering.

"And he will have eternal rest when the end occurs," Godwin said, his voice deathly calm. "But what if his death breaks reality further? Or if we get hounded by rioters? We won't always get a lucky break."

I froze, and I noticed something within the guard's eyes. He was wincing with pain, trying to escape.

"Do you think they are aware of their pain?" I asked, a lump formed in my throat. I watched him twitch, the blood always fresh, yet he never seemed to pass out from the bloodloss. If it wasn't for the wall you would have thought he was trying to flee from a tight space. But he was in pain. I could see it in his eyes, or perhaps I was wrong, were they ever even able to feel?

I beckoned Godwin over, he obliged with a grunt. I jabbed an eager finger at the man in the wall.

"This man is writhing in agony!" I exclaimed, not hiding my excitement.

"Even if he was, what could we do? He doesn't know this is the end, he is just stuck in the wall."

"Hey, what do you think you're doing?" the guard replied, as if some cheeky scamp was trying to steal some lemons.

"He doesn't know what is happening to him, he cannot understand his suffering," Godwin said, his voice glum.

I gave a weak nod and left the guard twisting and struggling in his stone coffin. A wave of disgust rose within me, he didn't know why he was in pain, entrapped in stone forever except in the deepest recesses of his mind. We just had no way of bringing that consciousness to the forefront.

I remembered Ashenfall being a lively city back in the day; a popular destination for the Celestial Visitors when they were around. People were always going somewhere, selling or buying something. It was once an economic hub for us, even more so than Eagle's Cliff.

Now, all the citizens were frozen in place, many in varying stages of decay. Their flesh was wasted as they became skeletal figures, unable to do anything or to stop smiling. Unable to move their arms to defend themselves. The city was now at a standstill.

I should have put them down. The children, who should have been plump little beasts were now malnourished statutes, frozen in whatever they did before The Broken infected them. They could not stop smiling, even as their faces became gaunt.

"What kind of God does this to people?" I said louder than I intended. "What monster does this to children?"

"A god that doesn't care," Godwin responded through a grimace before releasing a sigh. "Let's get going and get our supplies, there is nothing we can do for these people."

I knelt in front of a child, ravaged by starvation; a living skeleton holding his hand out, begging for food.

"Say something. I know you are hungry, say that you are, and we can feed you,"

The boy didn't move, didn't speak, but the more I looked into his eyes, I could have sworn I saw them bulge at the mention of food.

Godwin placed a hand on my shoulder, his voice strained to the point of breaking. "There is nothing we can do. We must go now!" He shouted the last sentence.

"Fuck you for letting these kids starve to death!" I yelled and stormed off into the city. Godwin said nothing, I didn't look back.

I marched through the streets, boiling with rage and feelings of uselessness. I cursed the Gods for their cruelty with gritted teeth. "Fuck you disgusting monsters, you sick, deranged tyrants!" I wailed, repeating those words over and over again.

Once I had left the city entrance, I was alone, the Broken townsfolk had seemingly gathered in one single location for whatever reason. The cobblestones beneath my feet cracked, it was real. The houses, all identical two-story homes with thatched roofs and brick walls, all painted from the same pool of white, blue, black, and brown. Repeating forever. My brain stung, and I tried to search through my memory.

I could have sworn the cobblestone pattern repeated after a certain point. My relief came, however, when I saw the general goods store. A distinct building with beautiful front windows displaying wares, not the usual one or two windows on the upper and lower floors. It was coloured a gentle gold, with a sign swinging in the nonexistent breeze. It was different, unique, and named The Warm Cauldron. I ran inside, eager to get the supply run done.

The manager waved stiffly in my direction. "Welcome to the Warm Cauldron. What can I do for you?"

"Not getting in my way would be nice," I said. I opened my bag and started scooping up everything I could get my hands on. Spotting a single bar of chocolate, enough for the two of us, I placed it inside my satchel.

"Welcome to the Warm Caldron. What can I do for you?" the manager said again, unbothered by the theft happening before him.

"The world is breaking apart; maybe you can help us contact the Gods. What do you think?"

"Welcome to the Warm Caldron. What can I do for you?" The manager said for the third time.

"No," I responded, stuffing a handful of nuts into my mouth before placing the rest of the can in my satchel; my belly satisfied I continued, "of course you wouldn't know what I am talking about. You can't even think outside your God-given script."

My satchel was filled to bursting; I turned around, drew my sword, and pointed it at the manager's throat. "Just say something that isn't in the script. Tell me you don't want to die by my hand," I said, arm quivering.

At that moment, with the sword against the man's throat, again I found myself staring at another copy of me. Just like the men in my regiment, smiling like an idiot, waving like a puppet. I was about to kill a version of my own flesh.

Rage flooded me; I wanted to slit the man's throat to free him from the hell we were in. To show to myself that I was different, I was not the same.

I didn't, however. I returned my sword to its hilt and stormed out of the shop. Godwin was right, we didn't know how reality would react to the murder of people, I didn't know how to react to my own corpse.

A sickening realization came over me; I was prepared to kill innocent people, children even.

I wanted to vomit up the nuts, but I kept myself together. The murder of innocent children and the power of mercy felt too cruel for that. *What would The Bringer think?* It was a thought that idly crossed my mind.

The anger simmered, boiling despite my best efforts and I slammed my fist into the wall of a passing house. The pain was real; the brick wall crashed my knuckles with a comforting crunch. I wrapped my hand in bandages, the blood that soaked them was real. I was real in this world. Within half a minute, the bandages would vanish, leaving my hand fully healed.

Nobody bothered me as I walked. I was utterly alone in the city, unaware of where Godwin was. The buildings of Ashenfall had seemingly clustered together like sardines packed in a can. They towered over me, forming barriers of brick and thatch. The only major landmark, the Cathedral which was always in sight. It popped up above the homes piled on top of each other like an upright statue. Yet, the houses I passed gave the impression of the remnants of an existing civilization. Newly vanished from the world, leaving unimaginative carcasses for future societies to study.

Would there be anything left to study if we fail? I thought, still queasy from everything that happened since we got here.

After walking the deserted streets, I finally found a citizen, standing stock still in the middle of the road. Frustrated by their presence. I let myself bump into the man. A moment of rebellion against Godwin.

I expected the man to fall over, I didn't expect him to fall through the ground. He didn't resist or make a sound, he just fell through the floor.

I gasped and jumped back, fearing I could have fallen through too. But the cobblestone road he passed into didn't look any different to the one I was currently standing on.

I heard a very distant male scream, from deep within the ground, I could hear the death cry of a man unable to move or resist.

I turned around and walked back the way I came, back towards the front gate.

Nothing had changed and I was growing nervous. What *if Godwin had fallen through the Broken ground? What if he becomes infected with The Breaking?*

"Godwin! Where are you?" I shouted, "I have my supplies!"

There was no answer, but I could hear faint crying floating along the still air. The deep cries were unmistakably Godwin's, a certainty that I don't have the words to express, just a feeling in my gut. The townsfolk had remained where I had left them, just standing, waiting for the end. Godwin was incorrect in his assumption. They hadn't reacted badly to my accidental killing.

I followed Godwin's sobs, sliding in and out of the maze of decaying people. I kept my eyes on the ground, I could not bear to look at the children wasting away. As I made my way toward the crying, a new sound appeared. "Please, sir, can I have some more?"

It was a child's voice, a boy no more than ten. He slid towards me; hands outstretched in a frozen attempt at begging. He was all skin and bone, his unblinking eyes stuck in permanent sorrow.

"Please, sir, can I have some more?" The voice was garbled like he was speaking in water.

"Hallo love, care for some roses?" said a squeaky-voiced woman, head only a skull, joining in with the child. I ducked and jumped to avoid their advancement. My shield vibrated as it had for the monsters, I killed on the way to Ashenfall.

One by one, the city's people came alive, moving like statues being pushed by an invisible hand. Some still had skin on them, others were bare bones, pecked clean. They babbled as they swarmed me, some asking for help, others trying to sell their nonexistent wares, and others just wanting to talk. All were trying to touch me.

Panic rose within me, surrounded by rotting people cursed by a cruel and uncaring God. Before I knew it, I was slicing my way through the horde; distressed, contorted screams rang over the din. I was manic from fear. I slaughtered an entire crowd of sick people.

None of them had touched me, and for a moment I stared in abject horror at the carnage before me. Some of the bodies had already begun to sink into the ground, frozen as they were, unable to express themselves. Other victims had their limbs flopping about like recently caught fish, desperate to return to the sea.

I walked in a daze towards Godwin's crying, shaking my sword clean of the boxy blood. My head spun from what I had done.

I found Godwin sobbing at another general goods store identical to the one I had just visited, his face buried in the countertop. "There is no one else aside from the two of us. But what if I die? What if he does? I can't do this alone, not in this place."

I put a hand on Godwin's shoulder, "Are you alright?" I asked, feeling extremely stupid for asking such an obvious question.

Godwin, startled, leaped onto the counter aiming a dagger at my throat. His wet red eyes widened when he realized it was me, and he slipped the dagger back into his pouch.

"Sorry," he said, wiping the tears with a sleeve and climbing down from the table. "Please don't surprise me like that again."

I nodded, "Let's get out of here. Are you ready?"

"Yes," Godwin said, gathering his satchel and heading towards the front door. The shopkeeper continued to wave stiffly, bucket on head."

Ignore him, he doesn't know anything." A tiny smile crept across my face as I followed him.

However, as we were about to leave, we heard discordant shouts and the metallic clang of farm equipment crashing together. It concentrated outside the front door.

"What have you..."

We were met with the most bizarre sight; a crowd of human statues stood before us. They were frozen like when we arrived but were now occupied by the sounds one would expect during a farmer uprising. They clustered in front of Godwin and I, smiling, bowing, pointing, or walking in place.

We stopped and stared, both confused about what to do, but the crowd didn't react.

"Did you do anything?" Godwin asked, watching the crowd stand in front of them. Invisible knives and farm tools banged, and angry shouts came from smiling, unmoving mouths.

"I killed some people," I said to Godwin.

Godwin turned to me, eyes flared.

"Why would you do that?" he yelled.

"Because they started moving and trying to touch me!"

"You've caused a riot, you fucking idiot," Godwin said, turning back to the growing crowd. "They are going to hound us until we die."

The mob didn't move, and neither did we.

"We run?"

"We run. There are too many of them, and we don't know what they are capable of."

"All right, but where do we need to go?"

"To the cathedral; the next Guardian is there."

Godwin weaved his way along the wall to avoid the crowd; they didn't notice him, the benefits of an assassin.

I turned to follow Godwin and instantly felt a sharp metal object ram itself into my side.

I staggered and clutched at the injury, thankfully, it was not a deep wound.

The crowd turned like floating statues, watching my every action. I tried to move when another invisible object flew into my face.

I stopped, holding my head, swaying in a daze.

A hand grabbed me, followed by a flash of powder. Godwin pulled me out of the crowd's radius, and we ran down the deserted streets. Looking back, I saw the riot group standing perfectly still, floating behind us like fleshy sliding statutes.

"You know the way?" I shouted, the horde behind us was growing louder as we ran.

"Of course!" Godwin shouted back.

We darted through the streets as more of the populus, still as sculptures, began to pour out onto the street. They screamed obscenities while invisible weapons clashed around them like angry windchimes.

Godwin danced through them; no items were thrown, but getting close to the swarm hurt us. Cuts and bruises appeared in an instant we got within arm's length of them.

We ended up in front of a pair of gates to the cathedral, a mountain in itself. Its wondrous architecture was now lay ruined. Parts of the building were non-existent, finely sliced and taken out like a knife through a cake.

"All ready?" Godwin asked, looking at me for confirmation as the horde of flesh effigies bared down on us. They were clanging, screaming, and howling as they flew toward us.

"Yes," I said, and we pushed through the gate.

It flung shut behind us, the corpse frames swarmed around the fence, and their frozen forms jumped up and down in a mad eldritch frenzy. After catching a breath, Godwin and I climbed up to the Ashenfall Cathedral.

"Don't kill any non-hostile persons again," Godwin said.

I grunted in response, the buzz of rioters still in my head. "I didn't mean to; they were trying to attack me."

"This place, I think everything is wrong." Godwin's hands covered his face, his fingers tightening. "I don't want to die here, I don't want to be alone in this world," he continued in a tiny whisper.

"Godwin," I said, ignoring the mania outside the fence. "I am sorry for storming off like that, I apologize for how I have treated you."

Godwin sighed in response. His eyes betrayed a sheepish air. "I understand, this world, that mob," he pointed at the horde, "it gets to the best of us. But we must stick together."

"To the bitter end," I replied.

Now that we were outside the Cathedral, I could see that the cuts didn't even leave the interior behind; there was nothing, just a plain empty void sliced into the building.

Godwin, in front of me, pushed through before the words flashed and the announcer said:

The Red Castle

"Wait," Godwin stopped dead. He glanced around; the foyer was clean, finely waxed and smelled of peppermint.

Godwin walked out of the Castle. Dumbfounded; I sat cross-legged on the shiny floor and held my head in my hands.

Godwin came back inside and joined me.

"The outside is correct, but somehow, we are in a completely different part of the country. This is The Royal Court, it's two days' travel away," he said.

"So, what should we do?"

"Pray that the Breaking doesn't spit us out of this away from our destination?"

"Do we have a choice?"

"If only we had the hammer," Godwin murmured.

I climbed to my feet, groaning and grunting from the effort.

"Do you notice that our bags don't feel heavy?" I said, I just wanted to lighten the mood.

"I did," Godwin said, "sometimes The Breaking isn't too bad, I suppose." He said, a weak smile blossoming.

"Just remember, we will be facing more aggressive foes than yesterday." Then, not looking at me, Godwin continued with the air of a grin, "Please don't die."

I patted him on the shoulder and proceeded up the foyer staircase.

On top of the second floor's mahogany landing was a warm and comfortable campfire. The flame, however, was dark blue, like the sea.

I was going to question why the royal family had a burning campfire in the middle of the main foyer, or one that was blue, but reality didn't make sense to me anymore.

We each drank from our sunflasks, the pleasurable warmth of its sweet nectar soothed and restored our wounds. We sat down waiting for the sparks of the flame to transform into liquid, filling our empty flasks with the holy elixir. Or they should have. Examining them carefully I realized that I was still stuck at three full flasks with one empty.

"Oh Bringer," I sighed, "What have you brought on us now."

"I only have my full three," Godwin said, "But if required we can share!"

"So where should we go?" I asked. The many marble and oak passageways spread like a tangled mass of mad architecture. Just looking at them seemed to make them bend and contort further.

Godwin traced the air with his finger, "This way," he murmured, pointing at the third corridor.

"How can you be so sure?"

"Call it an assassin's gut feeling." Godwin gave a wink.

A sudden realization of a missed opportunity stung my gut. "Do you think we could have talked to the Celestial Visitor?" I asked with the leaden cloud of panic in my brain threatening to consume me again.

"Maybe, not sure if they would answer us, or ignore us like that Messenger you encountered. They might have had more reason to care, after all, they were supposed to protect us from evil. But I guess we'll never know."

The walls shone like a mirror, reflecting our distorted personages at us. The only sound aside from our talking was the tap and click of our feet on the floor and a strange dull hum in the distance.

"They couldn't defeat the Breaking." I said, the words leaden as they arrived in my mouth.

Godwin opened his mouth but closed it again. Eventually, he muttered. "There is always a way out."

"Changing the subject, where are the enemies?" I said, realizing how alone we were in the castle. "What Guardian are we supposed to face?"

"The Blasphemous King and Queen," Godwin said, holding his finger up. "I don't really know anymore though, remember that we are supposed to be in the Cathedral. Maybe the enemies have fallen through the world; maybe the Guardians will spin around in circles."

"Think that could happen?" I said, my heart rising.

"Yes, The Blasphemous King and Queen could just sink through the floor and die instantly," Godwin said. He had the look of smug joy that comes with remembering something important.

I trailed my hand across the ice-cold marble to calm my nerves. "Let's get there quickly; I can't stand the silence."

"Shall I sing instead?" Godwin said, giving a cheeky smile.

"Alright, do you have any glorious ballads in mind?"

"I think I do," Godwin said. He puffed out his chest and proceeded to sing.

Here we are, off adventuring.
Off adventuring, off adventuring
Who knows what we will find?
Who knows what we will face?
Whatever we do, we will find what we seek, what we desire.
We will strike down all that stands between us.
And when the day is done, we will have beer awaiting us back home.
Here we are off adventuring
Off adventuring, off adventuring

Godwin's voice was a deep baritone, echoing off the walls in a manner of a mournful ghost.

"Is that how it ends?" I asked.

"I made it up on the spot, I don't know." Godwin said, sheepishly scratching the back of his neck.

"You have a good voice," I said, not knowing what else to comment on.

"Thank you." Godwin beamed. "I could become a bard maybe, when this is all over."

I didn't want to say anything. I suspected we both knew deep down that we would not escape.

I heard a new sound coming from the end of the hallway. A heavy, rasping gasp repeated ad nauseam down the narrowing hallway.

"Do you know what that is?" I asked, dropping my voice to a whisper.

Godwin grimaced and said, "I don't know. It sounds human, I think."

"A Broken human, maybe?"

"Quite likely, but let's get out of the castle; better to be out in the open than cornered in here." We walked towards the noise, emerging into a large courtyard.

A beautiful garden of roses, daffodils, and apple trees was now stained a single shade of black; the plants had not rotted but were simply a charcoal colour as smooth as the marble but lacking any texture.

The source became clear to us; at the opposite end stood what were once horses. But now their limbs had become elongated, and human armour had grown to cover their twisted appendages. It occurred to me that when horses became afflicted with the Broken, they took on weird positions reminiscent of a praying mantis.

They stood perfectly still, breathing their steady, rasping breaths.

Upon seeing them, we immediately prepared for a fight, positioning ourselves behind one another, eyes focused on our soon-to-be attackers.

However, nothing happened. They stood there, just breathing, standing like stone.

"Why aren't they moving?" I hissed, heart racing, sweat beginning to trickle down my forehead.

"I don't know; maybe this is part of the Broken," Godwin answered.

"What should we do?"

"Let's move forward; the Guardian room is over there." Godwin pointed at a massive metal door on the far north side.

"They won't attack us at once?" I asked, still panicked.

"Let's try."

We both kept our weapons ready and gingerly walked toward the metal door.

The horses stayed in their place, staring at the floor, they didn't even notice us. The weapons their riders once wielded were held at the ready but never raised. When the Breaking occurred, the knights on the horses merged with them, no longer human but something else.

We kept to the centre of the broken courtyard, not touching the strange colourless flowers. We avoided the paving stones that spasmed in and out of existence—all to the tune of the breathing. The endless, grating panting.

The horse that guarded the door stood proudly before it, wheezing that horrid, grating, gasp.

"Godwin, open the door," I said. My friend nodded and slithered in between the mass of limbs. While waiting, standing stock still in front of the monster, I couldn't help but wonder if they were once like me. They appeared to be similar, the same rank and station before they broke.

Could I become that? I thought, my skin crawling as I investigated the Broken creature's inhumanity.

The doors creaked open, revealing the fog wall. "John, come to me slowly, let's not alert them."

Crying, metal slamming, and the thunder of feet came into earshot. Turning around I saw a pile of still bodies, the townsfolk from Ashenfall, still chasing us.

"Oh, Bringer!" I groaned, the horse-and-knight monstrosities began to animate, rasping and gasping before turning around to face me. The eyes burned with a fiery animal passion.

The swarm of villagers collided with the guards like a flash flood, both sides swinging and lashing out with wild abandon.

Godwin rushed towards me, flipping over and ducking under the mass of limbs.

I threw up my shield, the dome formed instantly, the impossible mass of creatures bouncing off it like hollow balls against stone.

When Godwin got close, I momentarily lowered the shield. The instant I did, hooves and pitchforks came crashing down around me. Pain flashed across all parts of my body, my head bashed this way and that.

I raised my shield again, the light guarding us both from the slaughter. My head swam, blood dripped from my forehead.

"Come on, the King and Queen are right over there!" Godwin said through gritted teeth. He dragged me forwards, my shield holding out as the two swarms clashed with each other.

My body screamed, pain seared through every vein and pore of my battered form. My clothes were soaked crimson by a cruel, unfeeling mob of unthinking monsters.

Once we were inside the relative safety of the fog gate entry, I lowered my shield. My legs buckled, Godwin catching me before my sorry form hit the floor. In a free hand he handed me my third flask.

My body slowly healed; I could have sworn it used to be instant. But I enjoyed the sensation of my flesh knitting itself back together. Some warmth in this cold and uncaring world was always welcome.

My wounds mostly healed. however, a deep scar tore across my chest. My hands and arms were shaking, and I swayed on my feet.

"Well, they are still fighting each other," Godwin said, watching the carnage unfold. He turned to me. "You got beat up pretty badly, will you be able to fight?"

"I drank a flask," I said, the shaking had ceased. I could stand properly now, "I only have two left."

"We weren't prepared. But we can be ready for the next fight." Godwin strode towards the door. I didn't want to look back at the death and destruction. "Are you ready?" he asked.

I nodded, the disgust at what I had done roiled inside me, I was a murderer and could have killed both of us. I was stupid, reckless and a failure to The Bringer. But I had to keep going. I could wash away all my sins once we were done fixing the world.

Godwin entered the fog gate, and I followed.

A throne room was before us; purple velvet drapes lined the golden walls, and extravagant pictures of a king and queen and their subjects aligned the interior towards the throne. The throne's left and right parts of the room beheld a pair of stained-glass windows.

Queen Justine and King Alistair: The Blasphemous Royalty.

Seated in the thrones was a man and a woman. The woman was gazing into a mirror. She stroked her red hair as arms within the walls thrashed around, attempting to assist her. A few faces were on the brick, wriggling mindlessly. The King, however, appeared normal, sitting in a manner that suggested a thoughtful and distracted headspace.

Queen Justine lowered the mirror to see the two of us approach them. "Usurpers!" she cried in rage. The arms and faces fell out of the structure, hitting the ground with a wet splat.

"Go forth, protect your king and queen!" Justine commanded, raising a hand before the doors around the throne room thundered open.

Priests on the ground floor marched in; their penitent whips lashed their backs, causing explosions with each strike as they walked. Strangely enough, the priests themselves did not seem affected by their Breaking.

On the upper floor, mages appeared, some already setting off lightning sparks.

"I will deal with the mages, you take care of the priests," Godwin instructed, dodging a volley of fireballs.

Then, the strangest thing happened. The heads of the priests and the mages burst, their wet bodies slumped to the floor gurgling, arrows growing out of their backs.

A humanoid shadow emerged and stabbed the king in the back. He tumbled to the ground, blood pooling around him.

We both stood, dumbfounded as Queen Justine's skin flayed itself with cuts and bruises. She slid over to a nearby window and was pushed out of it by an invisible force. Her screams, at first deafening, faded away until nothing. Each death a fountain of ones and zeros burst out, briefly coating the room before the mysterious voice shuddered through us:

Guardian Slain,

We waited, expecting something else to happen, but the battle was over before it had even begun.

Godwin slumped to the ground, "What in reality was that?" he gasped.

"I think our battle Broke," I said, a small voice echoing in the desolate throne room.

"I suppose this is a good thing?" Godwin asked, staring at the sinking bodies. There was a dreamlike hilarity to what had occurred; I couldn't help but smile at the madness.

The campfire rose out of the ground like a rapidly growing weed. It glowed with a beautiful warmth of life and hope, the only safety in a dying world.

"Well done," I said, feeling stupid saying it out loud.

"Thank you," Godwin replied, his voice numb, his eyes fixed on the fire, apparently hypnotized by the comforting blue flame.

"Shall we have a rest?" I asked.

"Yes," Godwin said, "and let us eat as well."

We went to the campfire, cooked some fresh rabbit, presumably taken by Godwin from shops, and drank warm beer. The drink was refreshing and rich. The meal and the fire all seemed so natural to me, yet I had just seen reality snap; people die without rhyme or reason. I saw the queen self-immolate against her judgment or ability.

"Godwin, do you think this food is real?" I said, looking at the roasted meat in my hand.

"It tastes like it, well-cooked if I might say so myself," Godwin said with a chuckle that came out too fast.

"Why were you crying back then in Ashenfall?" I said before chewing on another piece of rabbit.

Godwin heaved a sigh before continuing to eat. "Because when you left, I was surrounded by reminders of our constructed reality. How every whore I slept with was designed solely to do exactly what I wanted, how I have no idea if my memories are mine or created by the gods." He chugged down some more beer before continuing.

"I saw how The Broken was tearing apart everything and everyone in that city. And alone," he threw up his arms, "I couldn't take it." There was a pause as he wiped away some foam from his lips. "I'm sorry you had to see that."

"You saw me stare at the ceiling for days at a time. Not to mention witnessing me have a meltdown after discovering my copies." I raised a mug of beer in toast. "To us, survivors."

"Only we are left. We have to look out for each other," Godwin said, producing a weak tearful smile. He also raised his glass to me. "To survivors."

We both drank our beer, the smooth richness soothed my throat, delivering contentment.

Godwin chuckled, "Do you still believe? The Bringer and all that sort."

"What else is there to do?" I responded, head hanging low as shame bubbled up.

Godwin shrugged, "There is a god who doesn't think we are alive, god is real, it is not The Bringer though."

He was right, but my soul couldn't accept that. "I am not ready to let go yet. Sorry."

"No need to apologize;" Godwin shrugged, "it is easier for me than for you. Tomorrow, we should get to the Hammer." He nodded at me in a solemn manner. "We will need all the faith you can muster for that moment."

"Do you want me to get on my knees and pray to it?" I asked, an eyebrow raised.

"No, you just have to believe that the gods, or god, will listen to us."

"How would I do that?"

Godwin ran a hand over his face, squeezing his eyes shut. "I don't know; I am just trying to get both of us out of here."

"Thank you." I said, "I appreciate your efforts." We laughed, settled down with our bedrolls, and prepared to sleep.

"Godwin," I said, a memory suddenly jabbed into me. "I... I miss my father."

Godwin froze as if waiting for me to provide more details.

"I... miss going to the lake to fish with him." I brought my hand in front of my eyes, just to try and block the tears trickling down. "I hate the fact that I might never see him or my mother again."

"John," Godwin said, turning to face me. He wore a picture of grim determination. "We will contact the gods tomorrow; we will get them to fix The Breaking. And I swear I will get you back to your father."

I didn't say anything, there was nothing to say. We just hugged each other.

I gasped, and dug through my bag, finding the chocolate, I offered it to Godwin with a single graceful motion.

"Oh," Godwin said after a pause, his eyebrows raised in delight. "Thank you," he took the chocolate, unwrapped it and broke a piece off for himself. He then handed the open packet back to me.

"I saw it as I was looting a shop, and I just knew I had to take it." The chocolate felt cool and light in my hand, I popped a piece in my mouth. I savored the sweet richness, feeling the chocolate break down and dissolve.

"I am going to treat myself to so much chocolate after all this." Godwin said, licking his lips like a satisfied cat. "What do you think?"

I was about to eat another block of chocolate before realizing what I was doing. I paused and stared at it, I should have felt guilty, part of me still had that sting in my gut, the shame of indulgence. I have been luxuriating more than ever recently.

What if he is real? I thought, *what if I will be cast into the eternal flame once I die? Or what if the true Gods were responsible? Will they punish me for drinking, eating sweets, insulting their puppets?*

I had no answer to the puzzle, no matter how hard I wanted to solve it.

"What's the matter?" Godwin asked.

"I have sinned too much."

"How so?"

I drank, I ate this," I motioned the chocolate held in my hand as if it were a piece of rotten fruit.

"I have wallowed in gluttony," I said bitterly, head hanging in shame.

"John, I am sure that The Bringer will forgive you for saving the world."

"Do you think so?" I asked, the words burst out like a rush of water.

"Do you really think he is going to punish you for saving reality because you had a drink and ate some chocolate?"

"And if The Bringer isn't real?"

"Then you don't need to worry." Godwin said with a shrug. "The gods will decide our fates but I doubt they will be anything other than grateful."

I ate another block and handed the remaining chocolate to Godwin, who devoured it hungrily.

We sat by the fire, the cerulean flames crackled merrily, our bellies filled and content.

"Do you think I can become a baker?" I asked, thinking back to the food I cooked.

"Are you considering abandoning the faith?" Godwin asked, a wry smile across his face.

"No!" The voice was much louder than I intended. "Just something else to do, nothing that includes killing."

Godwin shrugged, "I am a simple man, I kill bad guys, I fuck beautiful women and drink myself to sleep. I don't think there is anything else I would rather do." He paused. "But if you ever open that bakery, I sure will be your first and most frequent customer."

"That's, very, touching, thank you." I said, "I am glad that you are here with me. I don't think I would have gotten this far without you."

"Neither of us could have come this far without the other," Godwin raised his beer mug, "Cheers to us!"

I raised my own, the mugs clicked together, beer froth sloshed over like a breaking wave.

After we drank, Godwin stretched out his arms and yawned.

"It's getting late, shall we go to bed now?"

The beer left me with a warm fuzzy sensation, like the pleasant rays of the sun on a spring day.

"Of course!" I slumped down to my bedroll and turned over. "Good night my friend," I said.

"Good night, John," Godwin replied.

The warmth dried up as I lay sleepless, my head flooded with tormenting thoughts of my parents. I stared at the blue flame, unable to stop thinking about my father and mother. Broken and twisted into something unholy and inhuman. The memory of their love, their humanity, sapped away.

Eventually I fell into a fitful sleep.

Chapter Four: Our Broken World

I awoke to the sound of distant rumbling, sweating profusely from a strange panic.

"Shit, Godwin! Godwin!" I said, seeing that he was still asleep. I shook him awake vigorously; dust was falling around us, the ground quaking, and the glass windows were cracking under pressure.

Godwin awoke with a start, "By the gods, it's happening!" he cried. We threw our bags together in a frenzy. The glass shattered, throwing shards all around us in a violent torrent, the throne itself collapsed like a sandcastle in high tide.

Godwin grabbed my arm, "Whatever happens now, we stick together!"

I nodded. The floor split apart; fissures fit to burst. The room's walls started to bend inwards like they were about to be sucked into something.

"Follow me," Godwin yelled, and we ran to the inconspicuous door across the room. Godwin pushed it open and dashed through. I was about to join him when I saw the opposite side of the room rip apart.

A massive swirling void met my gaze. As black and heartless as the Gods, it tore chunks of the world away, consuming it into its maw, advancing slowly with each mouthful.

I threw myself to Godwin, desperate to escape from the void.

The doors slammed shut behind me, revealing a vast foyer draped in golden silk along the white marble walls. A low whisper drifted through the building, suggesting a hushed Liberian conversation. Finally, our strange narrator declared:

Ashenfall Academy

Godwin cried tears of joy. "We made it!" he said. He was jumping up and down before giving me a hug, which I dizzily accepted.

"We have time; if whatever that is, is happening in the Red Castle, then we should have enough time to get to the center of the Academy."

Pushing him off me took some effort; he wanted to hug me longer.

"Yes, of course," Godwin said, and he let go. "I am just so happy we have made it this far." We started our journey with a brisk walk, him with an arm draped over my shoulder.

"I am so happy to be fighting alongside you, John." Godwin said, "You here makes me want to keep going."

"Same to you, Godwin," I said. A smile grew on my face. He returned it.

Once we left the foyer, we found ourselves in a lecture room. No one was inside. The dust-soaked chairs sat in near darkness, made all the more impenetrable by the mist of dust.

The lecture room floor was a circular design, surrounded by high walls of stacked chairs upon balconies. The lack of ground floor doors gave the impression of a steep man-made cliff side.

"Fuck, I suppose we will have to climb up?" Godwin said, eying his surroundings. He fanned the arrant particles out of the way. "We would have to find something to use as a ladder?"

"What about my shield? I asked.

"It could work, I suppose."

A low hum, sounding like someone in the middle of prayer, made its presence known to us.

"What in the gods' name-" Godwin started before the sudden crash of chairs and tables interrupted him. Wood splinters flew everywhere like little daggers along with a cloud of powder.

From the platform stood a priest, head bowed solemnly in prayer, much like the ones with the King and Queen. One hand repeatedly made the cross sign while the other held a whip.

As he muttered another hymn, he slashed the weapon, but instead of in front of him, his arm snapped backward, hitting himself, and an area around the priest exploded, leaving destruction in his wake.

"Another one?" I whispered. The priest didn't notice us.

He murmured in a cold monotone, unintelligible to us.

He whipped himself again, and the walls collapsed around him. He fell, landed perfectly on the ground like a cat, and started walking towards us undeterred.

I threw my sword at the priest's head. It hit him square between the eyes, causing him to topple backward before collapsing. The familiar ribbons burst forth, sending debris flying. After waiting a moment, I strode over to the priest and wrenched out my weapon, bloody from the corpse. Wiping it against my leg, the cold sticky liquid dripping down to the floor sent a shiver. I returned my sword to the sheath, watching the wretched priest sink into the floor.

"Not bad John," Godwin said, impressed by my feat.

"Remember that we cannot let those priests get close to us alive," I said before realizing the compliment. "Thank you," I answered after a pause, "now let's climb up this place; maybe we can get to the Guardian."

Godwin nodded, "I think we should be quite close. We have time; we have time."

Godwin continued to mutter the phrase as he climbed. It was like a mantra to him. Hope and motivation pushed him to continue, at least, I had assumed as such.

Once we were on the upper floor, Godwin examined the room, mostly destroyed now, for a suitable exit. "Over there," he said, pointing at another door.

"Is that the shortest route?" I said, feeling the crunch of wood under my feet. My muscles were beginning to ache, and a fog of wariness was falling upon me. I didn't know how much further I could keep going, not with the void maw on the horizon.

"Yes, as long as reality behaves itself," Godwin said, striding towards the door. He pushed it open and peeked inside.

"Good news, reality is behaving itself." He said, beaming with joy.

We entered an extensive library, filled from floor to ceiling with books everywhere. Reading tables and chairs dotted the floor. The urge to read the books, regardless of how utterly useless they would be, crept into me. Oh, how I wanted to read them, take them with me.

But I didn't. Godwin kept up the pace for me, marching forward through the otherwise empty library.

I jogged up to him. "Godwin, did you ever learn how to read?"

"Very basic stuff, enough to understand contracts. But not much else."

I searched through my memories. Looking for any indication that I was taught to read. But nothing came to me.

"I wish I was taught how to read," I said. "I didn't even realize this until now. I never considered reading once in my life."

Godwin looked up at me with a smile. "If you want, I could teach you?"

"Teach me?" I asked.

"After this is over, I can teach you how to read," Godwin said, grinning.

"I, I would love that, thank you, Godwin." My stammering voice echoed across the room.

"Don't mention it," Godwin said.

A crack of thunder rang out within the room, the sound bouncing off the bookshelves. We both saw it then. The Messenger.

The Messenger was killing mages; people that we might otherwise have had to fight. They toppled over, fried by the lightning emanating from The Messenger's fingers. Godwin and I watched in awe as the final mage fell, screaming their weird scream. Their corpses joined in the undulating mass of their fallen brethren.

He was helping us; he knows what we are up against. But he must know that our salvation is on the way.

I rushed towards The Messenger and again performed the required action. "Messenger, I am grateful for your assistance in this dire time. Please, bless me with strength, or anything you see fit."

The messenger cocked his head. His brilliance blinded me from reason. "Please," I begged, tears forming in my eyes. "I have served The Bringer for so long. Please grant us power over the Guardian."

The Messenger gave a metallic grunting sound and thrust out his left hand.

"John!" Godwin yelled from behind me. It was too fast for me to react.

A tidal wave of force slammed into my body, sending me flying into a bookcase. Pain shot through my back; books and wood piled over me.

"John!" Godwin yelled again as he tore the rubble off me, panting more from fear than exertion.

I didn't move, I didn't want to move. My entire body was limp, a puppet with its strings cut.

"John, The Messenger or whatever it was is gone now. We have to keep going, we're almost there!"

"You, you go; I will just stay here," I said, defeated, remaining slumped in my position, my bleeding forehead only made me drowsier.

"No!" Godwin shouted. He grabbed hold of my collar. "I didn't get this far just for you to decide to die! We started this journey together, and we will end it together!" Godwin yelled; rage etched in the pulsating veins on his face. "Don't give up now; we have much to live for after the fight. Then, of course, we can escape from here and live somewhere, but there is something worth fighting for, John."

Godwin cupped my head in his hands and looked directly into my eyes. "Don't give up; push forward a little more. The Guardian are waiting for us a little further up the path." He then plucked one of his flasks and poured it down my throat.

I strangled back the welling tears and hugged Godwin. The pain eased away, my wounds vanished, I was able to stand again. "I will share my flasks with you Godwin." I whispered.

"Food can heal us too," Godwin said. He dug into his backpack and produced an apple, biting into it with relish.

We let go of one another, without looking at the vibrating, twisting, and bending corpses. We marched towards a giant pair of ornate wooden doors waiting for us, promising our salvation from this hell.

Godwin led the way to the door on the marble steps. He stumbled, and his foot fell through the floor as if it were made of air.

Godwin screamed, twisting around and grasping the floor that swallowed the rest of his body. "John, help me," Godwin shouted. I dropped my sword and shield and ran, falling to my knees before the squirming Godwin. Only his hands and head were visible on the floor.

I snatched up Godwin's right hand and pulled; his other arm reached up and grabbed mine. "Is there anything you can use to boost yourself?" I asked, straining from the weight.

"No, there is nothing, no solids or anything!" Godwin said, holding on for dear life as I pulled, groaning from the effort.

Something in my mind clicked.

I let out a savage roar, golden light bathed me in a warm righteous glow. I wrenched back, and Godwin was dragged out of the pit, back onto solid ground.

Godwin rolled over onto his back, panting and laughing. "I was wondering why you didn't use your powers in the past." He said, choking back laughter.

I roared again, my sword and shield flew into my hands, and I leapt towards the doors, landing with a flash and thud outside our destination.

The light in and around me faded. I slumped on the ground, dazed by what I had achieved.

Godwin got his feet and dusted himself off. He produced a rope, attaching it to a dagger. He threw across the floor, embedding it in the wooden door. He tied the rope to a supporting pillar, vaulted onto it, and ran across the rope. Jumping off it beside me. He removed the dagger and wound up the string.

"Thank you," he said, hugging me. *Nobody is left except for us; we have fought the world: We need each other.* I thought.

Godwin patted me on the shoulder, "This is it. Let's get this done quickly."

I returned the pat, still warm with hope and camaraderie. "We do this together," I said.

Godwin pushed open the doors, revealing the all too familiar fog wall.

"What Guardian are we facing now?" I asked.

"It should be The Arch Mage of Ashenfall, but I can't say that is what we will face for sure," Godwin said, his voice grim. He marched into the fog wall, into the unknown future.

A long ornate hallway stretched before us, walls constructed out of opulent glass, telling the story of The Guilty Betrayer. The floor was made of marble, finely polished as always. The glass barely hid the pitch-black mass of Broken land outside.

We walked in silence, our footsteps the only sound left in the world. The first glass panel showed The Bringer, a humble man from an unknown village creating a wooden chair.

"We're back in the cathedral," Godwin said, utterly befuddled.

The next frame showed The Bringer using the white flame to heal and feed the sick. He brought joy to everyone, except the people of darkness.

I remembered the story; it was the tale of The Bringer and his betrayal.

The next frame showed The Guilty Betrayer, a greedy and jealous man who was paid by the corrupt priests.

"I think we are facing The Guilty Betrayer." I said.

The frame showed The Bringer drowning in water after being delivered into the hands of the cruel and violent occupiers. He was mournful as he drowned, but also confident of his ascension.

A groan emanated from the end of the corridor, getting closer to us with each step.

The next frame showed The Bringer rising from the water, three days later, a brilliant white fire surrounded his nude body, the priests were on their knees, begging for mercy along the riverbank.

A raspy human shriek shook the hallway. Heart throbbing in my chest, I raised my shield and stepped in front of Godwin.

"You kill it, I protect you," I whispered to him.

"Thank you, my friend," Godwin said, and we continued forward.

The final frame was The Guilty Betrayer hanging from a tree, his insides being torn out by demons as he suffered his punishment.

We entered a large room, and a mass of chairs lined the floor, leading to a large coffin at the end of the room.

An organ began to play a low, mournful melody that I remember being used at funerals. The top of the coffin flew open and landed on the floor with a dull thud.

Nothing appeared; we didn't stir. Our weapons were ready. "We *are* going to face the Betrayer," Godwin said with more certainty.

Out of the coffin rose a sight that struck panic into my soul. Something so Broken and twisted that I could barely bring myself to look at it.

A corpse dressed in moth-eaten rags floated up. His neck bent at a ninety-degree angle which contorted from one side to the other at such a speed that his head was a near blur. The constant cracking of the neck made it even more sickening.

His body hung limp under the hangman's noose. His stomach was a mouth pulsating in a manner that suggested hunger.

We heard that all too familiar voice proclaim:

The Guilty Betrayer.

"Shit," Godwin said. "This one will be difficult."

"Any suggestions?" I asked; The Guilty Betrayer leisurely drifted towards us, the organ playing its sad tune was punctuated by the neck snaps.

"Throw things. If you can reach him, attack him directly," Godwin said, dashing off to my left. I locked eyes with the Guardian, *What sort of attack could it use?* I wondered. It didn't carry any weapons or anything that would be used as tools of combat.

The Guardian was now a foot away from me. A white flame dome encircled me, my mind raced through my options, waiting for the Guardian to attack.

How do I fight this thing? My mind was racing, my breathing getting raspy.

A wet, sticky sound came, like an animal carcass being cut open. The Guardian's stomach opened, revealing a black void in the corpse, out of it fired a volley of black ribbons with crimson ones and zeros etched onto them. My shield, fortunately, blocked the attack; the force had the power of a spear.

I remained poised and instantly slashed The Guilty Betrayer in an upward slice. The Guardian howled in pain; a hollow, hoarse cry that was distinctly inhuman. The sound dug into my head like hooks into tender meat. I gritted my teeth despite ringing in my ears.

"Keep that shield up!" I heard Godwin say. I did so. The shield itself erupted outwards, stretching like a weird platform.

Daggers flew past me, before clattering to the floor, hitting nothing. Something heavy fell on me, and I collapsed under the weight, discovering that the Guardian had dropped on me.

The shield shrunk back into its original form, leaving me exposed.

It groaned and moaned, neck snapping again, the Guardian bent its spine backward at a sickening angle and screamed. The belly opened before I could react. The ribbons cut through my armour, slicing into my flesh like a hot knife in butter.

Letting out a scream, I tried to grab a sunflask. The Guardian mercifully lifted itself off me at that moment, allowing me the time to drink from the bottle, knitting most of my flesh back together. It floated away to do whatever it was planning next.

I clambered shakily to my feet, hissing in pain; the scars burned through my poor body. I observed the room, trying to find the Guardian.

Godwin skipped around The Guilty Betrayer, dodging whatever came out of its belly; daggers flew, bubbling with the poison used to take down the Archmage, each hit accompanied with a sickening sizzle.

Putting my shield away, I raced towards the Guardian with my sword raised in both hands, white flames erupting out as I prepared for the attack.

After receiving another flurry of daggers, the Guardian bowed, snapping its back with an audible crunch in Godwin's direction.

Godwin was lifted off the floor by an invisible rope. He hung, hands gasping at an ethereal cord around his neck, choking.

Godwin gargled, his eyes bulging and turning blue.

I hurled my flaming sword at the Guardian's head. It sliced right through the creature and landed with a clatter on the ground.

That did the trick as Godwin fell to the floor, coughing and gasping for breath. A large hole bored through the Betrayer's head, a fire blazing momentarily.

The Guilty Betrayer jerked towards my direction. "Catch!" Godwin said, tossing the sword to me before drinking a sunflask. His second one.

Sword in hand and shield raised, I waited. The Betrayer readied an attack and charged. Leaping out of the way at the last second, I turned and began slashing and stabbing with desperate abandon, flames sparked and flared against the decomposition.

Godwin leaped up and grabbed the Betrayer's legs. Like a monkey he scuttled up them, stabbing the Guardian in the back. The Guilty Betrayer bent its spine at such an angle that its feet and hands faced the floor.

Godwin lost his grip and hit the ground with a thump.

Circles of pure black grew like fungus across the pristine floor. The circles began to erupt into black ribbons spreading widely within the radius. Godwin was able to move out of the way in time. But my legs became entangled in the mass of ribbons, slicing at my ankles. Tearing out of the ribbons, I fell over, my feet hurting badly. *Fuck, fuck* I thought, my body howled in agony as if I was about to lose my mind. I drank down my second flask as I saw The Guilty Betrayer return to its original position.

It focused on Godwin, slamming itself into him; the stomach attempting to devour him. Before it could, Godwin rolled away. The Guardian screamed in animalistic fury, instantly charging back into the fray.

I threw my shield at The Great Betrayer, and it slammed into the creature's back, embedding itself within. With my ignited sword in hand, I threw it at the creature's head again. It staggered back on impact. The blade, for some reason, stayed within the skull. Not that The Guilty Betrayer noticed either wound.

Godwin used the shield and sword to clamber up and stab the Guardian in the head. The sword and shield fell out of the corpse, clattering down. I scooped them up and slashed at the creature's legs.

I tossed my last precious flask to the bloodied and battered Godwin. He caught it with catlike ease and drank.

"Cheers!" Godwin yelled.

The Guilty Betrayer screamed again, bending over to repeat the earlier action; Godwin flipped around and stabbed The Betrayer in the heart.

Rolling out of the way of the circles, I saw Godwin, splattered in blood, ignoring the ribbons growing out of the Guardian's belly.

"Godwin!" I said before a ribbon tentacle lashed out at me, smashing into the side of my head.

I stumbled, the helmet preventing most of the damage. My head spun; I didn't see the circle bubbling under my feet.

Godwin jumped off The Guilty Betrayer before delivering a flurry of daggers in his wake.

The tentacles erupted from the ground, tearing my flesh apart. I ripped my arms free and was pulling my legs out when I heard a scream mingling with my own.

Looking up, Godwin delivered the final blow to The Guilty Betrayer. It collapsed, screaming and gurgling, before sinking into the floor.

The ribbons disappeared and I fell to my knees, bleeding profusely from my limbs. I tried to move, but my legs were no longer working. I was bleeding from my middle, my throat flooding with blood.

Godwin dragged himself to me. His left leg limp, cuts and bruises covered every inch of him.

I sat on the floor next to him. I was not saying a word, waiting for the announcement:

Guardian Slain

The sound sang our victory to us in joyfully bitter triumph. Godwin put an arm around my shoulder. "Well done, my friend," he said, swaying back and forth as if drunk. "The doorway should be open now." He took off his satchel and produced bandages and food, massive amounts of food.

He began to stuff the food into his mouth, pausing only to wrap bandages around his legs.

I proceeded to do the same.

"It will be slow, but until the blue flame is fixed this is the best we have."

I nodded in agreement, mouth too full of nuts to answer properly.

My legs screamed when I stood up. Godwin winced as he moved. He pointed at a door that had appeared at the far end of the room.

"I guess we will keep going until we get to the Archmage of Ashenfall," Godwin said with a gulp.

"I don't think we can do that," I said. "Will the trick you pulled work?"

"I still have the food, and if worst comes to worst, I think I still have the traps on me!" Godwin said, his face twisted with pain whenever he moved but he still had the strength to smile.

"We did well there," I said. "I wouldn't have been able to do this without you Godwin."

"I am glad you came with me through all this."

The rumbling was growing louder; the building was shaking, and dust started falling from the ceiling.

"Shit, it's here!" Godwin yelled.

Godwin stumbled, I scooped him up into my arms and ran, teeth grinding into dust. I ignored the pain, the screaming agony in my legs. I wanted to collapse. I was going to collapse. But I didn't, I kept going. A door had appeared behind the coffin—a typical worn wooden door.

I tried to kick in the door but instead, I fell right through it.

Godwin and I tumbled into another room. Dazed, my head screaming, I pushed my body up again. We had gotten so far that I had to keep going for Godwin. I had to save myself and Godwin. Nothing else mattered now.

The room looked familiar, the same library, the same wide-open space.

"The Archmage of Ashenfall!" Godwin gasped; I helped him to his feet. Godwin used me as a crutch until he could stand properly. I provided him with more food.

With a pale face, Godwin produced his final flask, he tipped back, a brief gulp before handing it to me.

"There's half left." He said, "Please drink it."

The rumbling had stopped, and all was quiet aside from Godwin's laboured breathing.

"Where's the Archmage?" Godwin whispered. The hair on my neck stood on end.

"I don't know... he might be gone, or dead." I said hopefully, before consuming a handful of nuts. The pain was ebbing away with the speed of a glacial iceberg. I was healing, just not fast enough even with half a flask.

Godwin sighed, from dread or relief I was not sure.

"Just as well, I know where to go." Godwin left my support and shuffled, his right foot lame, towards the place where he fell through all those days ago.

It felt like years to me. Just one long journey that blurred together.

His hand carefully pressed up against the nondescript section of the wall. His hand passed right through. He turned to look at me and nodded in confirmation.

We walked through the wall like it was nothing but air, ending up in the tiny dark room filled with thin green lines of numbers, chiefly ones and zeros. In the centre of the room floated a glorious hammer made of gold and bronze, it spun slowly in place.

The rumbling was growing softly again; the room shaking but holding for now.

"Shit, what now?" I asked, my eyes stinging from the sweat.

"Just keep talking; this is where they will hear us!" Godwin said, grabbing the hammer in one hand and pointing to the walls with the other. The walls which echoed his sentiment ran like a stream.

Godwin instantly started shouting, "Help, help, save us!" I joined in, grabbing the head of the hammer and yelling the exact words as Godwin. Our voices visually imprinted themselves on all surfaces of the room and hammer. The strange room bent and twisted. One moment we were on a mountain, another time at the bottom of a draining ocean. The room would become crowded with humans before vanishing in the blink of an eye. Animals, owls, and the laughter of humans rang out; bears roared, and horses flashed in and out.

We kept screaming, begging the Gods to notice us amidst the chaos born from the hammer.

Walls made of steel grew out of the ground around us, creating a thick prison. For a moment, all seemed quiet. But then the roaring void pushed back, and we were trapped in a tiny pitch-black room, with a hammer that we had no idea how to control. A strong smell of iron, freshly smelted and sulfuric, lingered in the air.

We didn't dare to let go; I was too afraid to, in case doing so would sever the connection we might have made. Godwin didn't do anything; he kept his eyes focused on the hammer as if it would teleport both of us out through sheer force of will.

"Any ideas?" I asked, my breathing heavy and deep from the thrill; I wanted to be happy, maybe I had believed enough, and soon the Gods would make themselves known.

There was a cracking sound; the door behind us bent inwards, and the rumbling resumed, drowning out all other sounds. We screamed and yelled at the top of our lungs for anyone to notice us, to hear us.

A muffled snap occurred, the walls and door flew off, light revealing the swirling consuming maw of the void. There was nothing to hold onto; the walls were smooth, and there were no cracks in the floor to grab. Godwin fell over and slid towards the maw.

"John, John, help me!" He screamed, hoarse with terror as he frantically looked for anything to grab onto.

I watched Godwin fly into the void, crying out as he vanished. The maw continued to devour the last remnants of our universe.

I closed my eyes.

As I felt my body fall into the void, I remembered all the good times I had when I was alive. I thanked the Gods for freeing me from our Broken world.

Chapter Five: The Time the Game was Alive

4th of November 2034

Gabriel Oliver: Well guys, it's done. *Elfoen Online* is dead and buried.

Raphael Carpenter: At long fucking last whoo hoo ◇ Free finally from that shit fest!

Michael Fox: At least we got the salary before the end.

Gabriel Oliver: Am I the only one who enjoyed working on the project?

Michael Fox: No! I loved working on the AI, we just were in over our heads and naive. We should have started on the RPG sooner rather than now.

Raphael Carpenter: We had no idea what we were doing, and honestly it was a slog, why did Emmanuel Hoffman think it was a good idea?

Gabriel Oliver: Who knows, I am just glad I have a job, Lazarus Software is safe thanks to him.

Michael Fox: Has he said anything about the project?

Raphael Carpenter: He never does, just tells us what we need to make and then leaves us be, weird honestly.

Gabriel Oliver: Eh, if we can work within the deadlines given by him, I fail to see the problem.

Michael Fox: Anyway, I shall be logging off and spending time with my children. See you next week!

Raphael Carpenter: I am going to have another drink and veg out in front of the tv!

Gabriel Oliver: Good night, guys!

Michael Fox: Good night

Raphael Carpenter: Good night

23rd November 2034

Gabriel Oliver: Guys, I think I might have found something.

Michael Fox: What is it?

Raphael Carpenter: Why are you messaging me on a Saturday??

Gabriel Oliver: I was going through some of the *Elfoen Online* text dumps today

Raphael Carpenter: Again, on a Saturday??

Gabriel Oliver: I was bored!

Michael Fox: ☹ What's up Gabe, it can't be that important surely?

Gabriel Oliver: So I was going through the text dumps and I found something rather interesting.

Raphael Carpenter: Well, spit it out then!

Gabriel Oliver: Did you guys when you were playing *Elfoen* that day see anything odd, like a thief and a knight acting strangely?

Michael Fox: I remember a knight coming to me in Eagle's Cliff and praying.

Raphael Carpenter: Oh god that knight ruined my time killing shit

Gabriel Oliver: I am going to be sending both of you an email, I think you need to read this.

Raphael Carpenter: Alright

Michael Fox: Beats watching tv I suppose.

Gabriel Oliver: What do you think?

Michael Fox: You sure this wasn't part of the programming?

Raphael Carpenter: No, this was never written, we never thought about the NPCs reacting to our angel avatars.

Michael Fox: Shit.

Gabriel Oliver: Are you thinking what I am thinking?

Raphael Carpenter: It can't be. If it was then we have killed two people...

Michael Fox: It's impossible, no way we created life!

Gabriel Oliver: I am going to talk to Hoffman on Monday!

Michael Fox: @Raphael Carpenter I want to go over the text dump with you again please.

Raphael Carpenter: Okay, okay.

Gabriel Oliver: I am going to try and contact Mr.Hoffman.

Raphael Carpenter: What on earth will he do?

Gabriel Oliver: I don't know, I think he needs to know about this.

Raphael Carpenter: Alright, suit yourself.

26th November 2034

Michael Fox: We didn't make any of this

Raphael Carpenter: Nope, none of this was in the script, or the programming

Gabriel Oliver: Did we kill them?

Michael Fox: No we had no idea!

Raphael Carpenter: 100%

Gabriel Oliver: We can restore the world right?

Michael Fox: We have no backup!

Raphael Carpenter: I thought it would save money!

Gabriel Oliver: Fucking hell! What are we supposed to do?

Michael Fox: Has Emmanual answered? Maybe he saved a copy of *Elfoen Online*?

Raphael Carpenter: He never answers!

Gabriel Oliver: We really did kill them, didn't we?

Michael Fox: NO we didn't!

Raphael Carpenter: How the fuck could we have possibly known we had created life??

Gabriel Oliver: Why didn't we pay attention?

Raphael Carpenter: We never stopped to watch them....

Don't miss out!

Visit the website below and you can sign up to receive emails whenever Stuart Tudor publishes a new book. There's no charge and no obligation.

https://books2read.com/r/B-A-NCJV-UQGBF

BOOKS 2 READ

Connecting independent readers to independent writers.

Did you love *Our Broken World: The Fourth Nightmare*? Then you should read *Black Masquerade: The Third Nightmare*[1] by Stuart Tudor!

Barbara's engagement party was supposed to be the best time of her life; surrounded by the best that life can bring in the 1920s, all she could think about was having fun. However, all that changes when a sinister presence with dire warnings of death and misery infects the house, branding everyone inside.

Black Masquerade is the third novella in the *Eight Nightmares Collection*—a series of stories about exploring the dark and fantastical. This story is about 70 pages long.

Read more at https://linktr.ee/stuarttudor.

---

1. https://books2read.com/u/31VkWa
2. https://books2read.com/u/31VkWa

About the Author

Stuart has been devouring stories since he was little, a habit cultivated by countless bedtime tales. It was during his high school days in 2015 when, after reading The Strange Case of Dr Jekyll and Mr Hyde and playing Fromsoft's Bloodborne, he began to appreciate horror. He has always been creating his own stories, reflecting his fascination with the imaginary. This motivation to write would quickly lead him to explore dark themes and settings.

His love of writing and horror would produce the Eight Nightmares Collection: A collection of stories about the dreamlike, the surreal, and encounters with the fantastical. An entrepreneur at heart, he has embraced the self-publishing route- delivering horrifying tales that will scare and thrill people the world over.

When away from the word doc, Stuart is studying for his degree in English or working in managing properties and real estate. If he is not doing that, he is taking a breather with a good book like Berserk, playing Baldur's Gate 3 or watching the latest Scream movie.

Read more at https://linktr.ee/stuarttudor.

Milton Keynes UK
Ingram Content Group UK Ltd.
UKHW021939281024
450365UK00018B/1176

9 798227 773937